I0819655

OBSTETRIX

YOUNG ADULT NOVELS BY

NAOMI KRITZER

Catfishing on CatNet

Chaos on CatNet

TORDOTCOM • TOR PUBLISHING GROUP • NEW YORK

OBSTETRIX

NAOMI KRITZER

This is a work of fiction. All of the names, characters, organizations, places, and events portrayed in this work are either products of the author's imagination or used fictitiously.

OBSTETRIX

Designed by Gregory Collins

A Tordotcom Book
Published by Tom Doherty Associates / Tor Publishing Group
120 Broadway
New York, NY 10271

www.torpublishinggroup.com

EU Representative: Macmillan Publishers Ireland Ltd, 1st Floor, The Liffey Trust Centre, 117–126 Sheriff Street Upper, Dublin 1, D01 YC43

The Library of Congress Cataloging-in-Publication Data
is available upon request.

ISBN 978-1-250-42337-5 (hardcover)
ISBN 978-1-250-42306-1 (ebook)

First Edition: 2026

Printed in the United States of America

10 9 8 7 6 5 4 3 2 1

TO MY DAD,

BERT KRITZER

OBSTETRIX

CHAPTER 1

I HAD A NIGHTMARE again about the trial, and woke up sweaty and angry, although the "sweaty" part might have been a hot flash. I lay awake in the dark, thinking about menopause instead of the trial. Were my symptoms bad enough to merit a prescription for estrogen? I thought about the speech I gave my own patients: every treatment comes with trade-offs. Side effects or long-term risks. You're the expert on *you*. What does your intuition tell you?

I finally gave up on sleeping again right away and reached for my e-reader. I liked to settle my mind at bedtime by rereading an old favorite, and I had been rereading a particular favorite over and over since I got arrested.

A few pages in, my eyes grew heavy again, and I set it aside and dozed.

I had to drag myself up when the alarm went off. It was a bright, cold winter day, the kind where even if there's nowhere for a draft to get in, the cold seeps through the windows and walls. Since I had a job interview, I put on makeup and did my hair. The scent of the foundation reminded me of the trial, too—my attorney had insisted I wear makeup every day, and also a dress, the more femme the better. Even though there, my intuition said I should wear a suit—something that said "doctor," that said "authority." I had deferred to her instructions. And, well. I'd gotten off, after all.

I had some coffee, checked my appearance one more time, did my best to shake off the lingering anxiety from the dream or the interview or both, and headed out.

THE INTERVIEW WAS AT a new maternity practice, associated with an even newer maternity hospital, built to solve the problem of obstetricians leaving the Dakotas. If you had the money, and especially if you had any sort of high-risk pregnancy, you could temporarily move to Minnesota and give birth here. Three big, ugly apartment buildings just north of I-94 offered spare furnished apartments; the clinic and maternity hospital ("All we do is babies, and we do it well!" announced highway billboards) were just down the road, with the top-notch NICU facilities of St. Paul Children's nearby, should anyone need them. The clinic was called MinneBaby, and to be honest, I *hated* this name, but fortunately I knew through the grapevine that everyone who actually worked there called it MB.

The MB clinic was in an office park, and I walked in through the main entrance, through a lobby full of heavily pregnant women, a few with toddlers in tow. A gray-haired woman in a white coat came out and waved when she spotted me. "Are you Dr. Elizabeth Gwinn?"

"Liz, please, but yes, that's me." I followed her back to a meeting room, where a circle of doctors waited for me.

The interview went fine, right up until someone asked why I left my last job. The first time this happened in a job interview I actually blurted out, "Didn't you follow the news coverage?" and it still threw me every time—*how are you an obstetrician who doesn't know about this? One state over?* But sometimes they knew and just wanted to hear how I framed the story, so I took a deep breath and summoned up my well-rehearsed answer.

"I spent most of my career in Minot, North Dakota. Last year I had a patient with severe treatment-resistant hyperemesis gravidarum. Her kidneys were failing, and I performed a termination, at her request. The prosecutor decided to make an example out of me and filed charges. I was acquitted after a trial, but I decided I didn't feel comfortable working in North Dakota anymore, so I moved here."

Light dawned. She *had* heard the story, but she hadn't connected it to me. "I thought that doctor—er, I thought I heard you went to work at the big abortion clinic in Illinois."

"They offered me a job, but I actually prefer maternity care. I just need to be able to take care of my patients to the best of my ability." Going on trial had been terrifying. Aside from my bitterness toward my home state, I knew myself well enough to be pretty sure that my clinical judgment would be impaired by my own desperate desire not to wind up in that position again.

"Doesn't the law provide some sort of exception for the life of the mother?"

"Well, that was kind of what the trial came down to. Whether my patient was sick enough for that to count. The prosecutor said that she had 'morning sickness,' like any woman with a wanted pregnancy would terminate for something they could have managed with saltine crackers or even Diclectin or ondansetron. My patient was in recovery from an eating disorder when she got pregnant, and she'd started out seriously underweight. She lost thirty-six pounds from the hyperemesis, and her labs showed her kidneys were failing. The prosecutor said the kidney damage I was seeing was from the anorexia rather than from the hyperemesis." It was quite possible that she'd started the pregnancy with compromised kidneys and not realized it. "The course of HG can be unpredictable, and the prosecutor pointed out she might have spontaneously recovered from it the day after I performed the abortion."

There were other reasons Maddy had wanted to end the pregnancy. This hadn't been planned. She'd wanted to leave her husband, not have a child together. She'd clawed her way back from full-blown anorexia to a fragile recovery, and she'd immediately feared that this pregnancy was going to cause her to relapse.

She'd begged me to terminate the pregnancy.

And then she'd testified against me. I don't know

exactly what happened between the day I performed the abortion for her and the day of the trial, but I'd heard she'd reconciled with her husband, and it seemed to have something to do with pressure from her parents. My lawyer thought the prosecutor had leaned on her, threatened to charge her criminally for the abortion as well, because on the stand she blamed me for not doing something else. Anything else. What else? How would she know, she wasn't a doctor, just a mother who would never hold her baby because I had taken it from her.

During the expert testimony on HG, I'd looked at the jurors. During voir dire, all the women had been asked if they had children, if they'd been pregnant, if they'd experienced morning sickness themselves. There was an older woman who had four children and two grandchildren who kept looking at me, her face set, and I felt a lurch every time she did, convinced that she was already planning to find me guilty. It wasn't like *what I did* was in any sort of doubt.

I was wrong about her. I found this out later, long after the words *not guilty* had sent shock waves down through my feet. She'd been the one who'd refused to convict me. Who'd held firm until everyone else had come around.

Another interviewer asked about my bedside manner and charting practices, and I was relieved at the change in subject. Then someone else went back to the trial. "You know a lot of the women we care for are *from* North Dakota . . ."

"I would be delighted to continue to care for women from North Dakota," I said. "My quarrel was never with the women of North Dakota."

"We'll be in touch," they finally said, and the woman who'd met me in the lobby walked me out.

Back in my car, I saw I had a text from my father. He still lived in Minot. When I moved to Minnesota, he'd come out to look over some senior housing options close to me, only to suffer a case of extreme sticker shock and go back to Minot and the little postwar bungalow where I'd grown up. And to be fair, his friends were all in Minot—mostly at the VFW post where he hung out almost every afternoon. How'd it go??? his text said. I'd told him about the interview during our weekly chat.

I decided this was too complicated to try to explain by text and called him back. "They're not going to hire me," I said.

"Oh, Lizzie," he said. (Only people who changed my diapers are allowed to call me Lizzie. Mom died in 2012, so at this point that means one person.) "You sound so sure, but you never think people like you."

"No, it wasn't that. It was the way they looked at me when we talked about the trial."

"That came up?"

"Dad. Of *course* it came up." I took a long breath and tried to sort out my perennial impostor's syndrome from my actual impressions of the interview. "They're going to come up with some reasonable excuse, like that my vibes were off, or I seemed a little cold, but the sad truth is, it's hard for doctors to admit that I didn't do anything *wrong*, and still wound up on trial for something I very definitely did."

"Doesn't Minnesota—"

"Abortion is totally legal here! But even here, other doctors want to convince themselves that it wouldn't have happened to them because they'd have documented their decision-making just a little bit better. Or sought a second opinion, or a third opinion, or talked to the ethics committee, or personally called up the attorney general of North Dakota to drop by the hospital, or who even knows, the point is, they want to believe that this could never happen to *them*, and that means they need a reason to believe that what happened to me was because I was a bad doctor."

My voice was getting a little ragged around the edges.

"You'll find something soon," my dad said.

"Belleville Options Specialty Clinic probably still wants to hire me," I said. "The weather might be better."

"You'd be even farther from home."

"Minot isn't home anymore, Dad. Not for me."

We sat there silently for a minute and I pulled myself together and said, "Well, I basically just called to vent, so thank you."

"Anytime, Liz."

"I'll talk to you Sunday. Love you."

"Love you too."

The phone rang within seconds, and I picked up thinking it was my dad calling back, but instead an unfamiliar voice said, "Dr. Gwinn? My name is Sarah Smith. I'm with the Prairie Spring Home Birth Collective. We're mostly midwives, but we're looking for an obstetrician to contract with and we heard you were looking for a job."

This wasn't anything I'd applied for, but I cleared my throat and sat up straight in my seat. "I am, yes," I said. "I don't . . . you do realize I haven't ever done home births."

"Right, right, what we're looking for is a physician to provide backup in cases where prenatal care gets a little complicated, but not in a way that rules out a home delivery—like if a woman needs a prescription for antibiotics, say."

Certified nurse-midwives *can* prescribe antibiotics, which meant this was probably a group of direct-entry midwives. You could get licensure in Minnesota to be a midwife without the nurse training, but I couldn't remember what sort of training they required for that.

"Where did you get my number?" I asked.

"Your coworker Jennifer in Minot." Jennifer was one of the labor nurses. I guess it made sense she might be friends with a direct-entry midwifery group. "Why don't you just come right now?"

"Wait, to interview?"

"I'll be honest with you, we want to hire someone quickly," she said. "I was thinking maybe if you came over and chatted, I could reassure you about us, and get just a little bit of a feel for you. . . ."

"I just finished a job interview," I said.

"Oh! . . . Well, look, I promise that if you get that job and leave us, we won't hold it against you. If you sign on for just a month, that'll get us out of our bind, at least for now. And you could probably continue part-time, if you wanted. . . ."

I thought about my depleted savings and dwindling bank balance—defense lawyers and expert witnesses and all the rest did not work cheap. My rent was due next week. "What's your address?" I asked.

Sarah sent me to a location in Minneapolis. "It's not going to look like an *office*," she warned, and she was correct: it just looked like a house. I pulled up and pulled out my phone to text her to be sure, but she was already out and waving at me. I put my phone away and followed her inside.

Sarah was younger than me, a white woman with light brown hair that some areas (not Minnesota) would say was blond, in a long braid down her back. The living room looked a little like it had been staged by a real estate company, with cheap but pristine furniture. "Have a seat," Sarah said, waving me at the fake leather sofa. "I'm going to get myself some tea. Can I offer you any?"

"No, thank you," I said.

"Coffee, then? Or how about a homemade soda? We just got one of those gadgets for the office that makes homemade soda, I'd love to show it off."

"Sure," I said.

"Do you like citrus flavors?"

"Sounds good," I said.

She returned with a cup of tea and a short glass of soda, no ice. I sipped it politely—it was fine—and set it down. "So I've looked over your resume," she said. "One thing that caught my eye was that you volunteered in Haiti?"

Doctors don't usually put their resumes up on LinkedIn—I'd done it on my lawyer's advice, ahead of the trial. "I did a residency rotation there, with a medical nonprofit," I said. "I've been back a few times with a group that specializes in repair of obstetric fistulas."

Sarah leaned forward with interest. "I knew another doctor who went there who said she learned all sorts of things doctors here generally don't know how to do. Like how to do spinal anesthesia."

"Spinal anesthesia is actually pretty straightforward,

but I wouldn't be able to do it for home births," I said, a little confused as to why she was bringing this up.

"Oh, of course not," she said. "I just thought it was interesting—doctors in the US tend to be so specialized. Can you tell me a little about your care philosophy?"

I started to talk about autonomy in choices, listening to my patients, empowerment. With horror, I realized that I was slurring my words. *What the hell,* I thought. I sat up a little straighter and took a deep breath, only to feel a wave of nausea.

"Oh my God," I said. The words didn't come out properly, and I thought, *They're going to think I'm drunk.* "I'm feeling sick. Is there—is there a bathroom?"

"Just sit there a minute," Sarah said, calmly, her hands cupped around her tea. "I'm sure it'll pass."

I'm not sick.

There's something in the soda.

I scrabbled for my cell phone, thinking, *I need to call for help, I need to call—*

The phone dropped from my fingers like wet spaghetti off a shaky fork.

THE WORLD DIDN'T GO dark, exactly; it went blurry. I was going through a list of likely drugs in my head, trying to figure out what they'd given me—Rohypnol? Chloral hydrate?—and realized I was doing it out loud. I felt the sting of an injection and my body went even more limp than it already had. *Muscle relaxant*, I thought, *or maybe another sedative*. "She can still hear us," Sarah's voice said.

The blast of cold outside air and then the musty smell

of a car heater. A too-cheerful radio voice talking about college basketball scores. The smell of burgers and fries.

A gas station, neon lit, sometime in the night.

I wasn't *playing* helpless at first, but by the time we arrived at the gas station, I was sufficiently conscious to think about trying to escape. I didn't know where we were, exactly, just that this was a gas station, so there might be other people around, and the car was stopped. I tried to look around, to figure out what I needed to do to escape my . . . I didn't want to say the word *kidnappers* in my head, but obviously I knew that's what they were.

I was in the back seat of a minivan, and no one else was in the minivan with me. I unbuckled my seat belt; that was obviously the first step. The door was a sliding door, and it didn't move when I tried to open it. I looked around for the unlock button; it didn't do anything. Would the window roll down? Could I escape that way?

"Sarah! You'd better hurry!" I heard a man's voice call from outside the car.

The door slid open. Even drugged up, I was determined to fight. I kicked out with my feet as hard as I could and heard an *oof* as I connected, and then I flung myself out of the car to try to run. Only, my feet weren't quite listening to me and instead of running, I found myself falling.

The asphalt was rough against my face and I struggled to push myself to sitting, but my body didn't seem to know up from down. My voice still worked, at least. "Help!" I yelled. "Help! I'm being kidnapped, help!"

There were other people at the gas station; I glimpsed a concerned face, but when Sarah and the man with her laughed apologetically and said, "Yeah, we're on our way to rehab for her, again," the face smiled in relief and turned away as the man and Sarah lifted me back into the car, buckled me in again, and drove away.

"That was too close," the man said. "I thought you said the sedation would last till morning."

"Well, it did," Sarah said. "She didn't *get* anywhere, did she?"

"Those people might remember us. If word goes out."

"Unlikely. Anyway, at least this way she can have something to eat." She turned back toward me. "You want some food? That's what *I* was doing while you were trying to make a break for it, getting you some *food*." She was affronted, like I was acting ungrateful.

"Is it drugged?" I asked.

"No."

She had a hot dog, a bag of Bugles, and one of those smoothie drinks that comes in a plastic bottle, which was, in fact, still sealed. And I was extremely hungry. She had water, too, and since that was also in a sealed bottle, I grudgingly drank it.

"Why are you doing this?" I asked, when I'd finished eating.

"We need an obstetrician," Sarah said.

My head was clearing enough now to think of alternate plans that I maybe should have gone with the first time, like stealing someone's cell phone and calling 911, but not enough to resist when Sarah reached back with another hypodermic syringe and injected something into my thigh.

It had to be more sedative: I wondered where they were getting it, whether it was from a pharmacy or a street dealer of some kind, whether they were calculating dosages or just estimating, whether they had naloxone if they were giving me an opiate . . . As I worried about whether they would even notice if I stopped breathing, the drug carried me off into a fog and I stopped worrying about anything at all.

THE BOOK I LIKED to reread at bedtime was one that I had first read in my teens. It was an obscure fantasy novel from 1985 that I'd found at my local library and checked out repeatedly, called *The Onyx Dagger.* I'd eventually damaged the library copy past repair—entirely by accident, to be clear; I'd had it in my backpack when my thermos came open—and a sympathetic librarian had told me that I might as well keep it. At my mother's suggestion, I'd put it on top of the refrigerator to dry, leaving it permanently stained but still readable.

That copy had eventually started losing pages, and after some hunting, I'd found a yellowed but otherwise pristine used copy to replace it with. More recently, the author, who'd only ever published a handful of books, put them all up as PDFs with a suggestion that readers could download copies and send her a donation via PayPal. I'd immediately sent her a hundred dollars, converted all the PDFs into EPUB, and put them on my e-reader.

The protagonist of *The Onyx Dagger* was a lost princess who narrowly escaped death when her parents were murdered by a necromancer. She'd disguised herself as a boy for a while, fled into the wilderness with her best friend, made new friends and allies through the purity of her heart and the power of her intense charisma, and finally regained her throne in a climactic battle involving a magic sword, a telepathic cat, and a conveniently timed dragon.

It was everything that made people trash-talk 1980s fantasy, right down to the map at the beginning that had locations like THE ENDLESS FOREST and THE MOUNTAINS OF DESTINY.

In the dim twilight of that endless car trip, I remembered a scene in which Deirdre, the protagonist, had to rescue her best friend Isabelle from a wizard who'd used mind-control powers on her. Isabelle fought Deirdre, but Deirdre knew that Isabelle was in there, that she wanted to be rescued. *Please come for me, Deirdre*, I thought. *I won't even fight you.*

"WE'RE HERE," THE MAN said. Brandon; I'd heard Sarah call him Brandon, sometime in the last day or two days or however long we'd been in this minivan. They hadn't let me wake up again fully enough to eat, and I was thirsty and very hungry. Sarah, bright-faced, pulled open the door and handed me bottled water and a bar of milk chocolate with almonds.

It was cold here; I was probably still in the northern US. The sun was low in the sky, and the air had the sharp note of acrid smoke you get on farms where they burn trash. We'd pulled in through a gate that someone was closing behind us. I thought it looked like a farm gate, the kind used to keep livestock from wandering, not something I couldn't climb over.

"We're twenty miles to anywhere much," Sarah said. "That's if you pick the right direction from the end of the driveway."

"You don't—" My voice was hoarse. I drank more water. "You don't have neighbors?"

"Not any closer than twenty miles."

"Let's show her where she'll be living," Brandon said.

Beyond a cluster of trees was a neat little . . . compound. That was the word that suggested itself to me. Probably they called it something else, like a town or a village. There were rows of little houses, reminiscent of Quonset huts, but with a pointy peak at the center of the roofline rather than just the smooth half circle of corrugated steel. The houses were small, with a couple of larger buildings down at the end of the row. Steel-clad pole barns stood beyond that. I heard a rooster making a ruckus somewhere in that direction.

They walked me up to one of the smallest of the huts and opened the door. "Ta da," Sarah said. "This is yours. We'll let you get settled in. When you hear the dinner bell, come up to the big building for dinner." She glanced at Brandon, then added, "Or if you want, someone will bring you a tray."

I stepped inside and closed the door, just to see if they'd let me. They did.

It was tiny but reasonably well insulated, and the heater was running; it warmed up fast. There was a door at the far end that led to a bathroom, and a closet with medical scrubs, new ones. I wear a women's L for the top and an XL for the bottoms, and they had provided the correct sizes for me. Also dresses, which I don't normally wear: two denim shirtdresses, with long skirts. I looked to see if they were my size and didn't find a tag; after a minute of confusion, I realized they must have been handmade. In the two-drawer dresser by the bed I found an unopened pack of black socks, an unopened pack of white underwear, two pairs of black thermal leggings, and an unopened pack of white sports bras, all the same respectable-yet-cheap brand.

I hated the idea of wearing their clothes, but I'd soiled myself while unconscious and my clothes were damp and smelled of urine. I undressed, showered—my skin was red and abraded from sitting in the wet clothes on that long drive—and put on clean clothes from the drawer, hesitating between the dresses and the scrubs.

We need an obstetrician. Had these people never heard of posting a want ad? But no: I could, in fact, guess their dilemma. There'd been an article that had popped up three times in my algorithmically curated news app, about how the last professional obstetrician had now left North Dakota. The doctor in the article was a younger woman who had grown up in Grand Forks and gone to medical school at UND. She hadn't gone very far—she'd just moved her practice across the river to East Grand Forks, in Minnesota. The article didn't mention my name, but the specter of my trial hung over the story like smog in icy air.

Patients in Grand Forks and Fargo could just cross the river to Minnesota, but as you traveled west through the Dakotas, the lack of obstetricians became more of a problem. And I wasn't sure quite where we were, but from my confused memories of the drive I thought we'd gone farther. Maybe west to Idaho. Maybe south to Oklahoma. Although the weather here seemed colder than I'd expect, if we'd gone south.

I put on a dress and leggings. The dress was long sleeved, and buttoned up the front to a rounded collar. It had pockets, although I didn't have anything to put in them. I washed my own clothes out in the sink and hung them up in the shower, then stepped back into the main room and poked around a bit more. No clock, no phone, no TV. No books. I checked the top drawer of the night-stand for a Bible, like I was in a hotel room: nothing.

They'd given me my coat when I got out of the car. Normally I had a pen, a little bit of cash, and a wad of random receipts tucked into my outer coat pockets, and a slim paperback tucked into the inner one. The pockets had been emptied, down to the spare quarters I kept in my pocket for the cart at Aldi. They'd left my hat and gloves, and as I went through the pockets I realized they'd missed one pen, a ballpoint that said MINNEBABY that I'd apparently walked off with after my job interview. So I had a pen, but nothing to write on. I tucked it back into the pocket where they'd missed it.

Who the hell thinks they're going to get good care from a doctor they kidnapped? I wondered. *What would they do if I just refused to lift a finger?* Most birthing women don't actually need much intervention; it's just that when you do need someone, you really need them. I could refuse to help. I could pretend to help and then do someone harm. Why would they expect me to do otherwise?

Some of the people here might assume I would provide care to my kidnappers because of the Hippocratic oath, but here's the thing about oaths like that: most doctors take them and then most of us don't think about them *all* that much. I'd taken a modernized Hippocratic oath in medical school, but when I was looking at Maddy's kidney function labs and listening to her sob, I did not think, *Not terminating this pregnancy would be a violation of my Hippocratic oath*; I'd thought, *Letting her continue to suffer would be wrong.*

Probably Sarah had figured I was a good bet because I'd risked prison to help Maddy. Probably that was why.

I DIDN'T REALLY WANT to go have dinner with the full population of the cult or whatever this was. But it would be much easier to drug my food again if someone brought it to me on a tray. So when the dinner bell rang—it sounded like an actual brass bell—I put my coat on and went back outside to trail after the rest of the crowd to the big building between the houses and the barns.

Inside, there were rows of tables and a cross on the wall. Children brushed past me as I paused to look around. The food was set out buffet-style and it smelled like lasagna. There was a hum of conversation, and everyone was openly staring at me. All the women and girls were in dresses, with long hair. There were about a hundred adults. Many of the women were visibly in some stage or other of pregnancy. Everyone here looked white.

Sarah bustled over when she saw me and showed me to a spot at one of the long tables. "Everyone, this is Dr. Elizabeth. Our new doctor!" There was a faint emphasis on *new*. Everyone smiled and murmured a greeting. I sat down, not saying anything. I was going to escape from here; immediate furious defiance was not likely to help me. I needed to regain my strength, let them think I was cowed, and be ready when the opportunity presented itself.

Once everyone was assembled, a bearded man rose. He looked older than Brandon or Sarah, probably around my age, and his beard was streaked with gray. When he stood, everyone got abruptly quiet. "Heavenly Father," he said. "We thank you for this fine food, and the community to eat it with. We thank you that Brother Brandon and Sister Sarah's quest did prosper, that you saw fit to allow this. Bless our new doctor, bless our community, we ask this in the name of Christ our Lord, amen." He then nodded in our direction. Sarah's face was bright and beaming. And then he sat, which turned out to be the cue for us to go get our food at the buffet. It was, in fact, lasagna, big trays of it, along with a salad of shredded iceberg lettuce and little bits of carrot. Someone was serving food: I was given a filled plate, but a lot of it was undressed iceberg lettuce. The lasagna was bland, but I had nonetheless eaten all of it even before the whole hall was done getting their food. I was hoping I'd be allowed seconds, but none were available. There was dessert: a small slice of carrot cake.

As I scraped the last of the frosting off my plate, I saw Sarah having some sort of whispered conference with some of the other women. She broke away and came over to me with a bright smile. "A baby's coming tonight," she told me. "Why don't you join me and the mother at our hospital?"

THE "HOSPITAL" WAS ANOTHER separate building. Larger than my "house," smaller than the dining hall, it had a bed for the laboring mother, two chairs, and a second bed, pushed up against the wall, that Sarah said was for me, if I wanted a nap. "Because labor can take a long time."

I washed my hands, more out of habit than out of a plan to do anything, and sat down. "What's your training?" I asked Sarah.

"I'm a midwife," she said.

"Are you a CNM?" When she'd pretended to interview me, she hadn't presented herself as a certified nurse-midwife, but the whole interview was a ruse, anyway.

There was a fraction of hesitation before she said, "I'm an RN with midwifery training, but not a CNM." The hesitation made me think she was lying about something, or hiding something, and I wondered what. Was she not really an RN? Had she not had any midwifery training? Maybe she'd been an RN, and had her license taken away. Given that she was a cult member who'd committed a kidnapping, anything was possible.

The laboring woman said, "Sister Sarah is a good nurse and a good midwife, but she can't do a C-section."

"Do you expect to need a C-section?" I asked her.

"No," she said. "Sister Joy's going to need one, though."

I blinked at her for a moment and then said, "You do realize I was *kidnapped*, yes?"

"Oh, yes," she said, serenely. "We needed a doctor really badly, you see. Because of Sister Joy. She's not due for another month and a half. I wasn't expecting a doctor for my birth, but I guess li'l acorn here wanted to be properly attended, since he waited."

"What do you expect I'm going to do for you, under the circumstances?"

"Absolutely nothing, Dr. Elizabeth! I'm an old hand at this. You can just take a nap over there while I birth this baby."

I did not nap, at least not right away. After that long drugged ride, I felt exhausted but not sleepy. I looked around the "hospital" instead, peering into cabinets and examining the equipment. "The narcotics are in that one," Sarah said, and held up a key. "I can show you what we've got, if you're curious."

I nodded. She got up from the bed, where she'd been rubbing the laboring woman's back, and unlocked the cabinet. Rows and rows of vials of clinical-grade morphine and fentanyl. "How much do you go through?" I asked, lightly.

She glanced at me, then away, her face reddening slightly. "We had an opportunity to stock up."

Locked up with the narcotics were two doses of methotrexate, which can be used to end a pregnancy but is particularly recommended for ectopic pregnancies. I let out a tiny huff of dark amusement when I saw that. Ectopic pregnancies got brought up at my trial, by the prosecution, as an example of the sort of abortion they would *not* prosecute for. On the bottom shelf: bupivacaine, which is the standard anesthetic used for spinal anesthesia.

Over on the bed, the laboring woman let out a low groan and then said, "This is going a lot faster than the last one."

From another cabinet, Sarah fetched an aluminum tank of nitrous oxide, assembled it with a mask, and handed it to the laboring woman. I'd heard of people using nitrous oxide for pain relief in labor, but I'd never actually seen it done. Women at the Minot hospital who wanted pain relief generally got epidurals.

I poked around through the rest of the cabinets while she rested between contractions. They had antibiotics, antiemetics, steroids, Pitocin. Bright lights that could be brought out and set up; sheets that smelled of bleach and disinfectant; Hibiclens, an autoclave, surgical instruments, an Ambu bag. Everything but the obstetrician, basically. I wondered how much of this they stole, how much they'd ordered. How much came from a legitimate medical supply house and how much from Amazon. Or Wish.

The woman groaned again, breathed in some of the nitrous, then let out a different noise, sort of a giggle, sort of a sigh. Well, they did call it laughing gas. She groaned again. I was pretty sure she was right, the labor was progressing quickly. She had the look of a woman in transition labor, the most painful part.

I ought to not care about proper anesthesia, I thought. These people *kidnapped me*, and even if it was Sarah who drugged me and Brandon who carried me into the minivan, the woman currently giving birth next to me was in on it and thought their need justified the kidnapping. If they had a woman they expected to need a C-section, they could have sent her to another state for the last month of pregnancy.

Unless she was also a prisoner here.

"Oh, *Jesus Lord, Lamb of God, Prince of Peace*," the woman wailed, across from me. She'd known about the kidnapping. She didn't need me. I couldn't be sure about Joy, but I could be pretty sure about her.

"That's right, Sister Grace Lynn," Sarah said. "That's right."

I lay down on the other bed and tried to take a nap.

When I was arrested for performing the abortion, they let me turn myself in and I thought I'd get bailed out right away. I was wrong. The prosecutor claimed I was a flight risk, because if I went to Minnesota, Minnesota might not send me back. The judge set bail, but he set really high bail. And between having to wait for the bail hearing, and having to wait for my father to talk to a bail bondsman, I was in the Ward County jail for six days.

The women in jail with me were a weird mix of people who were accused of doing stuff bad enough to be denied bail altogether (there was an alleged murderer in there with me—she was charged with killing her sister in an inheritance dispute) and people who'd done stuff that wasn't a particularly big deal but they'd failed to show up or meet their probation requirements or whatever, and now they'd been picked up on a bench warrant. Jail was very boring, and I'd listened to anyone who wanted to chat because it was a way to pass the time. There was a blond woman, young, who had been put on probation for identity theft and credit card fraud in Wisconsin. She'd left Wisconsin and moved to North Dakota and insisted, to me, that she'd *thought* she was allowed to do this. "Don't they want me getting a job and supporting myself honestly? Wasn't that the whole point of probation? I got a job! They've probably fired me now for no call, no show, anyway, but I *had* one!"

Dozing on the bed, I dreamed about the jail, and that woman—Grace Lynn's voice was a little like hers, and I dreamed that she was telling me about Wisconsin ("It gets so cold in the winter," she'd told me blithely—apparently she hadn't been through one in North Dakota yet) and then breaking off to shout, "In Jesus's name!" and, "LORD, hold me up, Lord!"

Even during my week in jail, it had felt like an absurd misunderstanding. The crimes I'd committed in previous years were all the sort of technical or accidental things you'd list out mainly to demonstrate how blameless and boring you were: I had once driven around with expired plates for four months, before noticing and paying for the renewal. I'd accidentally shoplifted garlic more than once, discovering the unpaid-for bulb in the corner of my cart as I was loading groceries into my car, and I always just chucked it in the bag without going back in to pay for it. I didn't always come to a full and complete stop at stop signs. Somebody like *me* didn't belong in *prison.*

The prosecutor had even agreed that I didn't belong in prison; he'd offered a deal. No jail time, I would keep my medical license, but I would have to issue a written statement saying that what I had done was not medically necessary, and I would have to counsel other doctors to "make better choices," I think that was the requirement. It was, honestly, a perfectly reasonable deal except that what I'd done *had* been medically necessary, and they wanted me to lie and say it had been wrong, and worse, they wanted me to tell other doctors not to do what I'd done.

So I'd refused. And it wasn't until we went to trial that the possibility I could actually spend *years* behind bars had sunk in.

GRACE LYNN'S BABY WAS born at 10:10 p.m.—I didn't have a watch, but there was a clock on the wall of the hospital, with a sweeping second hand for timing contractions. He was a healthy boy, born without complications other than Grace Lynn winding up with a perineal tear.

In addition to learning her name, over the course of her labor I'd learned that this child was going to be her fourth, although her second born in Harvest—Harvest was their name for the compound, which they called a ranch. Her favored boy name was Ozias, which apparently meant "salvation." She thought they could call him Ozzy for short. Her preferred girl name was Hosanna.

Sarah gave Grace Lynn her baby to hold and breastfeed, and encouraged her to push a little to deliver the placenta. I could not stop myself from looking over the placenta once it was out, to make sure there weren't any bits left behind; there weren't. Sarah washed her hands and gloved up to stitch the tear, and I was able to sit there and watch her inject local anesthetic and put in exactly one stitch before I said, "Let me do that." They do train midwives to repair first- and second-degree tears, but I know I'm better at it than most, and looking at Sarah's technique, I did not think this was something she'd been trained on by any nursing or midwifery school. I washed my hands, donned gloves, and took over. Sarah, fortunately, took the win without protest or comment.

I had not attended a birth since my arrest more than a year ago, and I hadn't really attended this birth, either—Sarah had. I was surprised by the rush of emotion I felt as I put in seven careful stitches. That rush of satisfaction at a job done with meticulous perfectionism, that was part of it. But also, I had *missed* this. And following that moment of sparkling joy of having this job back came a wave of anger that it had been taken from me, and that I was getting it back *here*, that I was caring for this woman because *I had been kidnapped and she had collaborated in my kidnapping.*

Despite that, I could do no less than my best.

Possibly I could do less than my best for Sarah, but she probably knew that, and anyway, she wasn't my patient.

When I was done, Sarah helped Grace Lynn clean up and dress, and she gave Little Ozzy a bath and dressed him and put a little knitted blue hat on his head, and finally went and flicked the light outside a few times. That turned out to be the signal that her husband could come. He was a big man with a thick dark beard who was pleased to hear he had a son. "We're calling him John," he said.

"I think Grace Lynn wanted the name Ozias," I said.

Her husband glanced briefly in my direction and said, "It's a good thing it's up to me, then."

Grace Lynn stood, a little wobbly, and took his arm; the baby, well-wrapped now, was tucked into his other arm. And off they went to their house or hut or whatever it was they lived in.

The clinic was very quiet now, and Sarah stripped the bed down, disinfected everything, and made it up again with fresh sheets from a drawer. "Who does the laundry?" I asked.

"There are washers and dryers in the community building by the kitchen," Sarah said. "Commercial-style. Hospital sheets get properly cleaned."

"This isn't a hospital," I said. "This isn't a safe setup for a C-section. Kidnapping me was a terrible strategy, even if I help you. That woman you mentioned, Joy, she'd be better off just spending her eighth month in some big city with a proper maternity unit."

"That's your opinion."

"I mean, sure. It's an *informed* opinion. You can hold a gun to my head and make me operate, if you want, but no matter how hard I try, I cannot turn this into a proper operating room."

"People survived surgeries in the 1920s," she said. "They survived surgeries in MASH units. You're not being asked to do brain surgery or an aorta repair. You're being asked to do a cesarean section, and this will be *fine*."

"And anesthesia? You don't think nitrous oxide is going to suffice for a cesarean section, do you?"

"Of course not. We have the equipment and medication for spinal anesthesia, and you—" She gave me a bright, satisfied smile that made me want to punch her in the face. "*You* know how to do a spinal. It was on your resume. You learned in Haiti. *I asked you about it in your interview.*"

The interview had receded into a drug-induced fog, but I remembered that question, and my answer. Which had not actually been, *I can totally do a spinal, I absolutely learned how to do that.*

But I could do a spinal; I had, in fact, done them during my rotation in Haiti. Also, spinals are pretty simple to do; if I refused to do one, the most likely outcome was that Sarah would do it instead, and that thought made me shudder.

She walked me back to my little cabin, and said, "You should probably get some real sleep. Breakfast is at seven, and you'll be seeing patients starting at eight."

I almost said that I might be *seeing* patients but that did not mean I would be *treating* patients. But we'd already established that I was not going to be able to sit on my hands if they put patients in front of me. And in any case, pretending that I was cowed and cooperative was more likely to give me an opportunity to escape than me being loudly defiant. I nodded at her stiffly and closed my door.

Inside, I was struck by a sudden suspicion, and went to the bathroom to check on the clothes I'd washed out and hung. When they kidnapped me, I'd been wearing my interview clothes: a wool-blend pantsuit in navy blue with a crisp dress shirt in coral, to make the outfit not look too funereal. The suit jacket had disappeared somewhere between Minneapolis and here, but I'd still been wearing the pants and the shirt, and had hand-washed both along with my bra, underpants, and socks. Every thread of clothing I'd meticulously scrubbed and hung up was now gone.

I sat down on my bed, breathless with a sense of betrayal that I recognized was, in fact, irrational. These people had kidnapped me. Why was I surprised that they had stolen my clothes?

I put on the pajamas they'd left for me, used the toothbrush they'd set out for me with the toothpaste they'd left in my bathroom, which was not the brand I used, and climbed between the covers. Normally I would read for a while once I was in bed. I pushed the thought away.

Staring up at the ceiling, I tried to put together what I knew. It was *cold* here—cold like Minnesota—and the trip had taken a long time, I was pretty sure it had been at least a day and a night. I kept thinking *Idaho*, but was I actually in Idaho? Hell, I might be in a state that *had* legal abortion and abundant obstetricians and this cult just wanted someone on-site. If you took a woman to a hospital, there were so many things the staff might report to the authorities, like if she was underage, or had injuries from abuse.

When will someone notice I'm missing? Will *anyone notice I'm missing?*

My dad would be concerned when I missed our Sunday phone call, but he did not even live in St. Paul, or anywhere near it. I hadn't given him the numbers of any of my neighbors, in part because I didn't much like my apartment and didn't think I'd be staying. I had no coworkers and no boss.

And adults were allowed to disappear. Back in 2015, one of my cousins—a woman in her mid-twenties—had gone missing. My aunt went to the police. Turns out there isn't a minimum twenty-four-hour wait, that's a myth, but they do want some reason for concern beyond, "I can't find her," because for all they know, you can't find her because she doesn't like you and doesn't want to talk to you. She and my aunt had just had a big fight, and she'd left and taken her purse and her car, and there was no particular reason to believe she was *missing* missing, other than my aunt saying she really didn't think her daughter would do that and not call.

And in Courtney's case, she actually was just really mad and taking a break from everyone, and she turned up a week later and it was probably good we'd just left her alone. She'd gone camping somewhere near Devils Lake and had turned her phone off and left it in the glove box, which to be honest would have been a perfectly lovely and healthy "get off the grid for a bit" experience if she'd told literally anyone that she was going camping, instead of just vanishing.

I hadn't had a fight with my father, but there were times I missed calls and didn't call back right away. He'd be worried that I missed the call on Sunday, but at most, I thought the cops in Minneapolis might go ring my doorbell and leave when I didn't answer.

Dad and I had talked about my cousin back when it happened. He thought she was probably just taking a break from her mother, because she'd taken her purse and her car, although he understood why my aunt was so worried.

"She might have started out taking a break," I said. "And then wrecked her car somewhere."

"Could happen," he said. "It's why you should definitely let me know if you ever take it into your head to go backpacking in Yosemite or something." He gave me an affectionate side-hug and added, "I would die of worry in your aunt's place, so don't you dare."

"I'd let you know," I said. "But you never tried to control what I did, after I turned eighteen." Unlike my aunt, who we all agreed was overprotective and controlling with her kids, especially Courtney, who was the oldest. "Even when I was a teenager, you kind of let me live my life. My nerdy, nerdy life."

"You did sneak out to that big party, your senior year," Dad said.

I looked up sharply, shocked. "You *knew* about that?"

"Our front door creaked. I didn't see any reason to worry your mother, so I let her sleep. I thought you were probably too smart to drive drunk."

"I wound up driving five drunk people home. It took forever. I thought for sure you'd be awake by the time I got in. I didn't realize you were awake when I went *out*."

"I know." He grinned affectionately. "I figured if I told you, you'd oil the door hinges."

It wasn't that I wished my father were as overprotective as my aunt. It wouldn't have helped, anyway. It was just that the more I thought about it, the more I had to accept the fact that no one was going to be looking for me for days. Maybe weeks.

I had to believe I was going to get out of here, somehow. I told myself that the people at the gas station had called the police, that they'd traced the license plate, that when I woke up this would all be over. I tried not to think about the fact that when Sarah introduced me, she'd called me "our *new* doctor," not "our new *doctor*." I wasn't the first obstetrician they'd kidnapped, and I did not think they'd needed a replacement obstetrician because they'd let the old one go.

CHAPTER 2

I DID FINALLY SLEEP, this time without dreams. Someone woke me up at dawn by banging on my door. There was a brutal wind whistling through the compound. I got dressed, put on my coat, and trudged to the gathering hall for breakfast, which was steam trays of pancakes and the sort of scrambled eggs that start as liquid in a carton. I don't much care for scrambled eggs, but I forced some down; it was protein. There was a big carafe of coffee, and I took some of that, too, and drank it black. It was absolutely terrible coffee.

As I was finishing the dregs and wondering if I'd need to drink a second mug of it just to get enough caffeine, the mother near me whispered to her child, "Hush now,

Pastor John is getting ready to speak." I looked up to see that the bearded man who'd led grace last night was rising, and everyone around me was bowing their heads. I gave up on the idea of going to get more coffee. Maybe listening would give me some clue as to what these people believed.

"Sovereign Lord," he began. "Our most righteous father in Heaven, look down on us, Your community, and bless us and our work this morning."

There was a chorus of people murmuring *amen*.

"We know how blessed we are—to be given *sanctuary*, to be given *holy work*, to be given *the opportunity to do Your will*. To have our children and our wives here, circled round by protection, hedged by prayer. Your guidance to us keeps us far from temptation, and we know—we know!—it's not just *temptation* out there. Satan doesn't just say 'come and see,' Satan says, 'come or else.' We don't know how long this Tribulation will last, Lord, but we are grateful every day, every *moment*, for Your guardianship of us. For Your guidance. My friends, I had a vision last night."

A ripple of excitement went through the crowd, and one of the women called out, "Praise Heaven!"

"Our Lord God sent to me a vision," he continued, his voice becoming less conversational and more dramatic. "I saw before me two little children. Two little boys, like enough to be brothers, played side by side in a field. And then a demon came toward the two of them. A terrifying demon, with poison fangs, and long claws, and sharp teeth, and I knew he was there to *murder* those little children. And I said, oh Lord, please—please won't You save them? I know it's within Your power, I know You can do it, just save these poor little children who haven't done anything wrong! And as I watched, an angel came down from Heaven and lifted just one of those little boys in his arms, and the demon cringed away from that angel, because he knew he couldn't have that one. But then he turned to the other child, and he *devoured* that little boy. Bit his head off like you'd bite into an apple. Tore his guts open with his claws. Glory be to God, we are the little boy who's being saved. The rest of the world will be fed to the demons—well, probably not the whole rest of the world, there are other Christians, other chosen ones, other people who are clinging to the true Gospel and keeping themselves separate, keeping themselves clean. But most of the rest of the world will be like that second boy, devoured. Us, we're the ones safe in that angel's arms."

Another chorus of *amen* rang through the room, more enthusiastic this time.

"And you know, sometimes it might feel tight, being held by God's messengers. Being protected like that. Sometimes it feels a little constrictive, doesn't it? You might look around and think, I'd really like to stretch my arms today. I'd really like TV again, or Internet. I'd really like some of what I gave up to be here. But remember—*always* remember—that angel is protecting you. Protecting all of us. Keeping us safe from the demons that would *tear us to pieces and devour our insides* given half a chance. That's the vision I have to share with you today."

He nodded at two women, who stood up with guitars and led a couple of enthusiastic songs that sounded like music from a Christian contemporary radio station, not like the hymns I sang at the Lutheran church services my parents occasionally took me to when I was a kid.

The sermon done, Pastor John brought up Grace Lynn's husband and their new baby, who was introduced to everyone as John. *You'll always be Ozzy to me, kid*, I thought. Then Grace Lynn's husband was given a Bible, which he opened to a marked passage. "Therefore, behold," he read. "The days come, saith the Lord, that they shall no more say, The Lord liveth, which brought up the children of Israel out of the land of Egypt. But, the Lord liveth, which brought up and which led the seed of the house of Israel out of the north country, and from all countries whither I had driven them; and they shall dwell in their own land. Jeremiah, chapter 23, verses 7 and 8." Everyone around me was listening with their eyes closed, I realized. They started opening their eyes as they heard "Jeremiah." After that came one more hymn, which was sung without the guitars and had a refrain that went "God is good!" with a bunch of rhythmic hand clapping.

"Go ye and do the work of the Lord!" Pastor John said, by way of benediction, and everyone started to make their way out.

I wondered if maybe I could go get another cup of coffee now, but Sarah had seized my arm. "It's time to go to the clinic," she said. "Our patients will be coming shortly."

I let her tow me to the entry where all the coats were hanging up; I had a brief moment of worry that someone else would have taken my coat, with the pen hidden inside. But my coat was on the hook where I'd left it, the pen still in my pocket.

That Bible, the one Ozzy's father had read from—that was the only book I'd seen here.

Outside the gathering hall, the wind had died down, leaving a damp, overcast sky. The hall was at the top of a little rise, offering a decent view of the compound now that it was day. There were two rows of houses facing each other across a gravel driveway that led up from the road, past the path up to the gathering hall, and on to the outbuildings.

A gust of wind from that direction brought the smell of hay and cow manure. It smelled like my memories of my grandparents' dairy farm. We'd visited out there regularly when I was little; it had been sold at auction when I was still very young.

Dad told me once that he'd joined the Air Force because he wanted to go to space, because the stars were as far as anyone could get from that farm, which he wanted to escape more than anything. For me, the smell summoned up memories of the pineapple upside-down cake my grandmother always baked for us during visits, accompanied by a glass of milk from Grandpa's cows, and the tire swing that hung from the tree outside the farmhouse. For my father, it brought back the feel of an ice-cold outhouse seat in January—Grandma and Grandpa hadn't gotten a septic system until 1961.

Sarah had paused at my side, following my gaze. "Do you have any experience with agriculture?" she asked.

I shook my head. "Not really."

"We do ranching here, but you won't be doing any

animal care. That's mostly the job of the men and the older boys."

"What do you raise?"

"Laying hens, and steers." She started down toward the clinic, and I followed her. Probably the smallest of the outbuildings was the henhouse. The others might house the cows for the winter—winter was calving season, I remembered hearing from my father. One might be hay storage, or other feed. One had to be agricultural equipment; maybe a car was in there, too. Something I could use to get away.

In the clinic, Sarah saw a series of women for prenatal checks. Most of the women had young children in arms or in tow, and Sarah handed the babies off to me while she examined the women. Little Ozzy got weighed without his diaper before he got handed to me to hold. I like babies—never wanted one of my own, but I'm quite fond of other people's—and I stroked his downy hair. The children here, they were blameless, even if every adult was in on the kidnapping.

I took a minute to look the children over as they passed through my care. They were generally well-fed, so there was that, at least, and the babies showed no obvious signs of abuse. Starting in toddlerhood, some of the children had marks that I would have absolutely needed to report to Child Protection if I'd seen them in my clinic in Minot. You're allowed to spank your children in North Dakota, but if you hit them hard enough to leave a mark visible later, that's abuse.

As an ob-gyn, I rarely had to make those phone calls. My friend Lori, now retired, was a pediatrician; she generally made one or two a month. It was rare that there was follow-up for anything less serious than a broken bone, she told me once. She'd have called for the red welt I saw on the chubby thigh of a toddler girl who smiled at me and then wiped her runny nose on my shoulder, but probably nothing would have come of it unless there'd been another welt, and another call, at the next visit.

All the women spoke in high, slightly breathy voices. I'd heard women speak like that before; Jackie, one of the younger clinic nurses, had once called it "Fundie baby voice." Not in front of a patient, thank goodness. I didn't much like the term; it was openly insulting, it was my job to take care of religiously devout women as much as any other women, and some women just have high voices. It's not inherently an affectation. Listening to patient after patient who spoke in that same artificially girlish voice, though, I grimly decided that Jackie had been right.

There were two sorts of mothers here, I noticed right away that first morning: the ones who had joined the cult themselves, and the ones whose parents had joined the cult and brought them along.

The ones who'd had a relatively normal upbringing were fully grown, mature women. Some had tattoos, although many were religious, like the woman who had "saved by grace" in cursive on her left hip, and the woman who had a decorative cross and "John 3:16" on her upper arm. They all seemed comfortable with Sarah—chatty, even.

The ones whose parents had joined and brought them along were strikingly young and much quieter.

Joy was the last patient of the morning, and definitely the second kind: a slight woman barely out of her teen years. She had fine blond hair and crooked teeth. For Joy, Sarah unlocked a closet and rolled out an ultrasound device and a laptop computer. She pulled up a bunch of earlier scans, and tilted the screen toward me so I could see them. Then Joy lay back, and Sarah pulled up an image of her baby.

Joy had a bicornate uterus, a fairly severe presentation of it, and the fetus—which was a little under twenty-eight weeks along according to Sarah's notes—was in a transverse lie.

There are a couple of ways babies can position themselves in the uterus. Vertex is what you want, if you're the laboring mother: head down, chin tucked, face toward the back. Sunny-side up babies are head down, but facing the wrong way—that position causes back labor, which is more painful, and can cause labor to stall. Then there are the various kinds of breech, where the baby's head is up and feet or butt are down. Usually we do C-sections for those, but I've delivered the occasional baby butt-first, most recently when a woman who hadn't gotten much prenatal care showed up fully dilated and pushing, and there simply wasn't time to do anything else.

"Transverse" is when the baby is fully sideways. You can't deliver a transverse baby vaginally, any more than you can stick a sideways cork into a bottle of wine. Sometimes you can do an external cephalic version to get the baby to turn, but not when the mother has a bicornate uterus. It's not safe. The only option is a cesarean delivery. This, clearly, was why they'd wanted me.

"You need hospital care," I said to Joy.

Joy looked at me, her eyes filled with a deep wariness I'd seen more than a few times over the years. It was the look of a woman who didn't believe any real choices were open to her. "You're all I'm going to have," she said.

"May I examine you?" I asked, and Sarah slid over to make space for me as Joy nodded.

I drew out the exam for a good long while, making small talk, trying to learn what I could from Joy. Her husband's name was David. They'd married two years ago and this was her first pregnancy.

"How long has the ranch been here?"

"Three years," she said. "Before that we lived—" She broke off and I was pretty sure she'd gotten a warning look or gesture from Sarah.

"Do your parents live here as well?"

"Pastor John is my daddy," she said.

"How old are you?"

"I'm twenty," she said. "David and I married on my eighteenth birthday."

"How did you find out you had a bicornate uterus?" I asked.

"When I didn't get pregnant right away we went to see a doctor in—we went to see a doctor, a ways away from here, and he did a whole workup. Said this shouldn't keep me from getting pregnant but might mean all sorts of things could go wrong."

"Did he determine the cause of the infertility?"

"Turns out it was David's swimmers. Not so good at swimming."

"Oh, really? And I bet they checked that last, didn't they, after they'd stuck you with a million needles and had you pee on every sort of stick ever invented."

That got me a hesitant smile even as I could feel Sarah stiffen behind me.

"Anyway," Joy said. "They had me lie with David's brother, Brother Calum; apparently there's something about that in the Bible."

There was, but only if David were *dead*, and I did not get a "widowed" vibe here, although I sure didn't get a "happily married" vibe, either. If she'd been my patient in Minot I'd have brusquely sent her husband off on some errand and asked a bunch of questions that finished with "Are you safe at home?" (If you just spring that question on women who aren't, some will tell you what they think you want to hear just to get away from you.) And regardless of her answer I'd have given her the number for the battered women's shelter along with my ten-second "some abuse doesn't leave bruises; they'll help you with that, too" talk.

David wasn't here. Sarah was, though. I came up with an errand for her, saying that Joy was too thin (she was, in fact, much too thin) and I wanted Sarah to go to the dining hall for some vanilla ice cream or some vanilla pudding right that minute, but she just rang a bell that brought a kid to the door, and the kid went running up to the dining hall for the vanilla ice cream, as instructed, while Sarah stayed put.

Joy knew the exact day of conception. I gave her a list of things to watch for, and told her that we should plan on a cesarean delivery at thirty-seven weeks. "And again, you should have that at the nearest actual hospital," I said. "Not here."

"Again," she said, "you're all I'm going to get."

She had the same high voice as everyone else, but with a weariness that made her sound much older than the rest.

As the door closed behind Joy, I felt the anger that I'd been stuffing down in favor of cooperation and survival burst through like stormwater cresting a levee. "That woman needs an actual hospital," I said, furiously, to Sarah. "She needs a facility with a crash cart and bags of blood they can transfuse into her if she hemorrhages. If you people cared about Joy you would be *planning a hospital delivery for her* and not *kidnapping an obstetrician*."

Sarah's head went back; her eyes narrowed. For a second I thought she was going to slap me across the face.

She did not. Instead, she put on her coat and handed me mine. "You are clearly still tired from your long trip," she said. "You'd better go lie down in your cabin. I'll walk you over there."

The lunch bell started tolling as we walked over. "I think you need rest more than food," Sarah said, tilting her head with a faint condescending smile. "Go get some rest. You can join us at dinner."

My stomach growled, but it wasn't as if I'd never missed a meal. This was . . . kind of like the slap she'd held back from. A punishment, but more a warning than a *serious* punishment. A slap said, "I can hit you. I can do whatever I want to you. I have power over you." So did depriving me of a meal.

I lay down on my bed—not that I was actually going to *sleep*, but there wasn't really enough space to pace—and thought about the fact that there was a *laptop computer* in that little clinic of theirs, a computer kept under lock and key. Was there an Internet connection somewhere?

Might there be times it was unattended? Sarah had put the key to the laptop cabinet in her pocket; could I get into it without the key?

In the late afternoon, there was a knock at my door, and when I didn't immediately answer, the door swung open anyway. "Dr. Elizabeth," someone called. It wasn't Sarah's voice.

I sat up. "What," I said, repressing the instinctive question *what do you need?* It was two men. Probably not coming about a woman in labor, then; the gender divisions here had been pretty stark, so far.

"I'm Brother Elmo, and this is Brother Calum." Calum: David's brother, the biological father of Joy's baby. Both of them looked young, not like children but young enough they'd probably get carded if they went to a bar. "Pastor has instructed us to show you something."

"Is Sarah coming?" I asked, not moving.

"She's busy."

I grabbed my shoes and slid them on, then put on my scarf, coat, gloves. They hadn't said where we were going, but they were both dressed for the cold. Brother Elmo, I noticed as I stood up, was carrying a hunting rifle over his shoulder with a padded sling. "What's that for?" I asked.

"Someone spotted a bear sniffing around yesterday," he said. "If we see the bear, it's for the bear."

There was not, in fact, a whole lot I could do about it if they were planning to murder me. I followed the two men out of my cabin and up the street, past the communal building, and then past the barn. "Where are we going?" I asked.

"Not much farther."

We ended at a tiny burial ground with white wood cross markers. "We haven't lost a lot of people," Calum said. "But the ones we did lose were mostly little ones. That was Sister Michelle's." He pointed at a cross. "That was Sister Holly's." Another cross. "We also lost Sister Ginny—she was a mother who was giving birth—and her baby too; they're in the same grave."

I started to relax, thinking that the goal of this trip was to persuade me that they had kidnapped me out of real desperation, but then Calum pointed to a final, unmarked grave.

"The doctor we had before, she chose not to save Sister Ginny. Brother Ethan, Sister Ginny's husband, he shot that doctor when she said she wouldn't help. Doc's buried there."

I stared at the grave. The wind suddenly felt very cold.

"You do realize that I could *try* to help a woman or a baby and they could still die," I said, my voice shaking despite my best efforts.

"You don't see a grave for Sister Sarah here, do you? We don't shoot folks for *trying and failing*. Doc Jana, she just wouldn't even try. We can go back now, this is what we wanted you to see."

They walked me back to my cabin, tipped their hats—literally, like characters out of an old western movie—and said, "See you at supper."

THE MEAL THAT NIGHT was chili and cornbread. The chili was heavy on the beans and tasted more like ketchup than like chili. There was honey for the cornbread, at least. I looked around the room as I ate, wondering which person here was Ethan. How long ago he'd murdered the other doctor.

Pastor John stood up to read everyone a chapter from the Bible after dinner. Like the reading earlier, it was in the ornate, archaic language of the King James Version, and it took me a minute to recognize the story of the Prodigal Son. When he was finished, I tried to watch to see where the Bible went, and spotted it: it went into a locking box.

Sarah and Calum walked me back to my cabin after dinner. "There's a social gathering tonight for the community," Sarah said, "but it's probably best you get to bed early. You've clearly got rest to catch up on."

When I opened my window briefly, I could hear music, faintly, coming from the dining hall—fiddle and banjo. I closed my window again; it was still bitterly cold. I took my pen out of my coat, pulled my mattress to the side, and made two hash marks on the wall. Yesterday, today. It had been January 12 when I was taken, two days . . . probably . . . of travel. I made a note of my best guess as to today's date. The two days, at least, that I'd been here—that, I was more certain of.

I tucked the pen under my mattress, and put the mattress back against the wall. Then I went into the bathroom for a drink of water, and looked into the mirror. I looked old; I looked scared.

That was the real reason the lawyer wanted me in makeup, I thought. Putting on those layers of paint helped me look like I was in control. Helped me remember to *pretend* to be in control. I had to present myself like I believed I would get off, like I trusted the jury. This . . . this was different.

I took a deep breath and thought, *I'm going to survive this.*

My eyes did not look convinced.

I'm going to survive and escape.

I was going to have to be patient. I was going to have to convince them that they'd cowed me—the more I cooperated, the more my captors would let down their guard.

"Sleep when the baby sleeps" was advice I always gave to new mothers. Sleep when the baby sleeps, instead of getting up and trying to get the dishes washed or the laundry folded. Prioritize your welfare, your healing. *I need to sleep when they let me sleep*, I thought now. *I need to eat when they let me eat.* I needed to be ready for the chance to escape when it presented itself; I needed to be patient until then, and prioritize my own welfare as much as possible.

My father did not talk much about the Vietnam War. In high school, I had interviewed him for a paper I was writing. He'd joined the Air Force because at the time, all astronauts were Air Force pilots. The fact that an ROTC scholarship would help pay for college seemed like a win-win. "I'll be honest," he'd said. "I absolutely thought the war would be over before I got out of college. The US entered World War II in December of 1941, and Japan surrendered in September of 1945. That was an entire world war we won in a little under four years! Surely by the time I was out of college, we'd be done in Vietnam."

"What would you have done, if you'd known we wouldn't be?"

He thought about that question. "I don't know. I wish I could say it would have mattered, but I was young, and dumb. And really pretty desperate to get off my parents' farm, and that was another thing, a military career was something my father respected, a reason for leaving the farm he'd accept."

In Vietnam, Dad had spent a year flying combat search and rescue missions in a prop plane, an incredibly dangerous job. He'd been told by another pilot after he arrived that he should just assume he was going to die during his twelve-month tour. He'd refused to accept that, he said. He thought that if he believed he was going to die, it would happen. He'd told himself he was going to make it through. That he'd survive and go home.

Dad had never gotten to be an astronaut. His eyesight had deteriorated; he'd been grounded, a year or two after finishing his tour in Vietnam. He'd survived that year, though. He'd gone home.

I looked at myself in the mirror, thinking about my father. "I'm going to survive this," I whispered to myself. "I'm going to escape."

CHAPTER

3

"SLEEP WHEN THEY LET you sleep" was all very well and good, but *falling* asleep was another matter entirely.

I lay in bed in the dark, thinking again about where I might be. If I was right about two days of travel, that would have taken me out of the Dakotas—unless Sarah and Brandon had taken me for a longer drive than necessary just to disorient me. But that stop at the gas station made me think they probably wouldn't have done that. Iowa, Nebraska, Wisconsin, Missouri, they were all within a day of Minneapolis.

I could be in Montana. Or Wyoming, Idaho, Utah, maybe Colorado. I reconsidered my conclusion that I wasn't in Oklahoma, but the buildings here seemed to have been built to withstand cold more than heat. It also smelled like boreal forest here, which excluded Nevada and made Colorado and Utah less likely. I could see hills around us; if there were mountains beyond, I couldn't tell.

I'd assumed at the start that they'd dragged me to a state where all the obstetricians were gone. That would exclude Washington, Oregon, and Colorado. But their real motivation might have simply been a captive obstetrician, so hell, maybe I was in Oregon. Did it even matter, if I was twenty miles from anywhere?

If I could steal a car, I could probably get away, but the cars were kept locked up. If I could find something with Internet access, I could send a message, but again, everything was kept locked up. These people even locked up the *Bible*.

I was going to have to be patient.

Trying to run too quickly could get me killed, or at least watched a lot more carefully. I needed them to believe I was cowed and cooperative. They'd showed me a grave with the intent of intimidating me—let them think it had worked.

Honestly, it kind of had.

Joy would reach term in eight weeks. If I was still here at the end of March, I would in fact need to perform a C-section on her, for her sake as well as mine, and hope for the best.

I thought about the man's comment about Sarah not having a grave. Did he mean that they'd murder one of their own members for shirking their work? Or was Sarah an abductee, like me, originally, with a raging case of Stockholm syndrome? I'd read an article years ago (because it came across my social media) about how Stockholm syndrome was kind of a myth, that the original Stockholm kidnapping victims had distrusted the police for good and valid reasons, and this seemed so inexplicable we'd made up a whole syndrome for it. On the other hand, Patty Hearst had been persuaded to commit actual crimes on behalf of her kidnappers. I couldn't remember what her captors had done to her, and my mind started circling through various horrifying possibilities if these people decided to try to brainwash me.

I sat up and turned my light back on. This was not going to get me to sleep. At home, I dealt with anxiety-induced insomnia, the kind where my brain took me on a tour of past traumas or spun up images of future ones, by reading. Especially rereading. Especially *The Onyx Dagger.*

I didn't have my book, or any other book, but I had reread the opening page so many times I could almost see it in my head. After a minute I turned my light back out, lay down, and summoned it up as best I could.

> *The cold wind brought the smell of snow, and Deirdre, red-faced from the cold, paused in the stable yard, breathing in a deep breath of it. "My lady," the page said. "Your father said to send you in, directly."*
>
> *"Oh, I know," she said, giving him a quick smile. "I promise I won't delay much."*

I couldn't remember the exact words that came after the opening but I remembered the scene: the traveler that comes thundering into the stable yard, hurrying past the princess into her father's audience chambers. Being sent off for dinner with her ladies. The decision to slip down and eavesdrop . . .

Wrapped in the familiarity of the story, I dropped into sleep.

. . . only to dream that I was in the Ward County jail, trying to call my dad. But the phone had no numbers on the keypad, and when in the dream I thought, *It's okay, phones always put their numbers in the same layout*, the keys suddenly multiplied so I was trying to dial his number on a five-by-five unmarked grid. "Hurry up," someone was saying behind me. "Hurry up! You're almost out of time—"

I woke with a gasp. It was still night.

I used my little lavatory and then put on my shoes and coat and stepped outside. I'd been wondering how closely I was watched, especially at night, and "I had a nightmare and wanted to take a little walk to clear my head" was a perfectly reasonable explanation for going out, if anyone asked. I let the door shut behind me to keep the warm air inside, and went for a walk up and down the row of houses.

Motion-sensor lights snapped on as I walked, but otherwise the compound was quiet and dark. There was one little hut down at the very end that had its light on, and as I walked a lap, a man came out of it; he met me back in front of my hut. I didn't recognize him, but I was relieved it wasn't Calum.

"What are you doing?" he asked.

"I had a nightmare," I said. "I wanted to go for a walk to get it out of my head."

"Okay," he said, and made a "carry on, then" sort of gesture as he sat down on my doorstep to watch me.

I did another lap. "Are you my minder?" I asked when I circled back.

"Not yours specifically. If a little kid went wandering in the night, that wouldn't be good. And if someone wakes up and needs help overnight, they can just call the night watchman."

"Is there a way I can call for you?"

He pointed at a little button like a doorbell just inside my door. "Use that."

I did another lap, but I was getting very cold. "What's your name?" I asked when I got back to my hut.

"I'm Brother Ethan."

My blood turned cold as I realized he was the person who'd killed the other doctor. "Oh," I said. "I heard about you."

"Yeah," he said. "Sleep well, Doc. It's four a.m.; you've got a while before the breakfast bell rings."

I didn't fall back to sleep, despite the words *sleep when they let you sleep* echoing through my thoughts like an accusation. The guard was the other doctor's murderer; he watched over the community at night, and the motion-sensor lights told him anytime someone was moving around.

I started thinking of possible ways to solve the problem of the lights. There might be power outages; I could bolt during a power outage. Of course, running around without a flashlight was a good way to get lost or injured, and running around *with* a flashlight was a good way to get found before I'd made it to safety.

I'd caught my father smoking on the sly when I was nine because a light, even a tiny light, is so easy to see at night. We had a park at the end of the street and he'd gone out for a walk. I wanted his help with a homework assignment and had gone out looking for him. He'd put the cigarette out by the time I caught up with him, but it was too late; I'd seen it.

I was *so mad*, because he'd pretended to quit months earlier, after I'd delivered a lecture on how I didn't want him to die of cancer. He told me it was hard to quit, and I didn't believe him, because all he had to do was *not light a cigarette*, how could that possibly be hard? *Hard* was things like memorizing the multiplication tables, a task I had completely failed at, to the exasperation of my teacher and both my parents.

My dad laughed and told me that if I would memorize my times tables, properly, by the end of third grade—which was coming right up, at that point—he would quit smoking for real. If I didn't, he wanted me to stop nagging him.

I had my times tables memorized two weeks later. My dad let me throw away all his cigarettes, and after that, as far as I knew, he'd never touched them again.

And because I'd finally jumped through that memorization hoop I was able to get into the advanced math class the next year, which led to the advanced STEM-track classes, which ultimately got me into med school.

It was kind of ironic I'd been so worried about the cigarettes. Something like half his friends from his years in Vietnam had died of cancer, not from cigarettes but from Agent Orange exposure. Dad was doing fine.

At least, last I knew he was doing fine.

That was a stressful thought, not a comforting thought.

All my escape plans assumed I'd be able to get away without freezing to death. I might have to wait until the weather warmed up, months from now. *And if I walk along the road they'll find me, and if I walk through the woods I might never make it out of the woods . . .*

I don't need to figure all this out right now, I told myself, and tried to sink back into the memories of *The Onyx Dagger* again. I managed to get my mind out of the "but if I walk along the road they'll find me, but if I walk through the woods I'll get eaten by a bear" circle that felt like my brain was on one of those spinning playground merry-go-rounds we'd had back in the 1980s, but I didn't get back to sleep.

In *The Onyx Dagger*, Princess Deirdre, among her many other adventures, is held prisoner for a while. It's doubly tense, in the book, because her captors don't know who she is; she's traveling incognito with her friend Isabelle, still disguised as a boy. Isabelle is recognized and taken away (that's when she gets hypnotized); Deirdre is kept with the common folk who've been taken prisoner. So she's not as heavily guarded, but she's also definitely viewed as disposable. She has to escape, knowing that if she's caught, she'll be killed out of hand.

When I realized I wasn't going to be able to get back to sleep, I replayed that scene in my head.

"As long as they haven't cast us into chains yet, there's still hope of escape," Deirdre whispered to her fellow prisoners. "But escape we must. They'll send us to the mines if we don't."

"At least we'll be alive if we're in the mines," one of the men said, angrily.

"For a month or two, sure. Better to die fighting than die of the sulfur fumes."

"We can probably get you away," one of the other prisoners said. "You're a young lad, your whole life ahead of you."

Deirdre let that tempt her for a moment, then shook her head. What sort of princess—what sort of queen would she be if she allowed her people to save her, and not themselves? There must be a way.

There must be a way.

Outside, someone rang the dining hall bell. There *was* a way, in the book, but it involved a telepathic cat. I hadn't even seen any regular cats here. I got up, dressed, and put my coat back on. I pulled the mattress back an inch and added a hash mark to my count of days. Then I went up to get breakfast.

"TODAY'S NOT A CLINIC day, just so you know," Sarah told me as I got myself scrambled eggs and a bowl of oatmeal. "You'll be staying up here after breakfast. Unless someone goes into labor, of course!"

"Or has some other health crisis?" I said. "I assume sometimes people get sick or injured?" Maybe they took those into town? But Sarah nodded enthusiastically.

"Last month, Sister Janet sprained her ankle. I used the ultrasound to make sure it wasn't broken and wrapped it. It'll be good to have a real doctor here."

There was a lot that could go wrong if you had an obstetrician doing your orthopedics. But honestly, we were probably far enough from the nearest hospital that if you had a doctor close by, you'd want them to do what they could even if it was just keeping someone from bleeding out while you called for a medevac.

I wondered if they'd get a medevac if someone like Brother Ethan had an accident with some farm machinery, or if I'd be what he got, like Joy.

"Anyway," Sarah said. "On Fridays, I help out in the kitchen and teach a fitness class." She laid out a list that had definitely been laser printed, so one more reason to think there was a computer around here somewhere. It was a list of tasks. "Of the highlighted tasks, which do you think you might like to help out with?"

I picked up the list. My first thought was to wonder what they'd do if I said *no*. But if I wanted to lull them, even a little, I had to cooperate. Also, the best case if I refused was that they'd pack me off back to my cabin and leave me to die of boredom.

Also, maybe I could get out from Sarah's supervision and try talking to some of the other women. See if anyone seemed like a good candidate for carrying a message.

I looked over the list. The cooking tasks were all highlighted, probably because Sarah could watch me herself. Most of the cleaning tasks weren't, probably because I'd be unsupervised for long periods. Knitting, hand embroidery, and custom beading were not highlighted but had a circle around them and a question mark. "Custom beading?" I asked.

"Can you do that?" Sarah asked. "We sell custom wedding veils on the Internet. I just assumed you probably wouldn't have learned to do beading."

"No, I was just curious," I said.

"The custom sewing is part of how we make money

for the community," Sarah said. "It's probably not worth teaching you those skills, though, because most of the time you won't be using them."

"No," I said, and scanned down a little farther. "Mending," I said, finally. "I stitch very neatly."

When breakfast and morning prayers were done, about half the tables got folded up and rolled to the side of the room, and the others got shuffled around. I was directed to a corner at one end of the room, where a set of folding chairs sat around a basket of damaged clothes, with a couple of bright task lamps plugged in to the outlet on the wall. I took a seat, found a needle and thread in the sewing kit, and grabbed a sock out of the basket. Other women were settling in near me. "You must be Dr. Elizabeth," one of them said. "We should introduce ourselves. I'm Sister Emma." The names went around: Emma, Janet, Heather, and Natalie. Natalie looked about my age; the other three were younger, probably in their thirties. Emma and Janet were mending clothes in need of repair; Natalie and Heather were hand-beading veils, attaching tiny glittering crystals to the edge of a cascade of cream netting.

"Do you know how to darn socks? Because I can show you if you haven't done it before," Emma said. "Don't just sew up the holes, that's a recipe for giving someone a blister."

"I darned a mitten once," I said. "I generally just replace socks."

"We have darning eggs, if you want to try, but let me know." She clearly didn't trust my darning skill, which, fair enough. I put back the sock and took a shirt with a seam that had given way. It had no tag and I was pretty sure it had been made on-site. Emma was patching a pair of boy's pants with a Carhartt label on the back pocket, though, so clearly they didn't make everything.

"Did you hear that Sister Grace Lynn wanted to name her baby *Ozymandias*?" Heather said as we stitched. I wondered if I should put in that she'd actually wanted the name Ozias, but decided to just listen. "Can you imagine?"

"Isn't Ozymandias in the Bible?" Janet said. "If it's a biblical name it seems like it ought to be allowed."

"Ozymandias isn't in the Bible," Emma said. "It's a poem. I read it in secular high school when I was growing up. Or—wait. Maybe he is in there, come to think of it. The poem's about a pharaoh."

"Right, there's a pharaoh in the Bible," Janet said.

Natalie cleared her throat and everyone fell silent. Probably no one would have wanted my helpful observation that Ozymandias was the Greek name for Ramses II, anyway.

I finished sewing up the ripped seam in the shirt I'd been working on and started to fold it. Natalie snapped her fingers and held out her hand in a "give here!" gesture, and I passed it over so she could inspect my work. She looked it over, brushed her finger over the seam, gently tugged to make sure my stitches wouldn't give out again, then nodded, satisfied. "You're not bad at this."

I smiled and kept my retort about learning to sew in medical school behind my teeth, but Emma glanced at me like she'd had the same thought.

"Sister Sarah said you're from Minneapolis?" Janet said.

"I didn't live there very long," I said. "I'm actually from Minot, North Dakota."

Janet sat up with interest. "I lived in Grand Forks for a while when I was a kid. My dad was in the Air Force."

"Oh," I said, immediately reaching for the obvious connection point. "Mine, too."

"We had to move to Illinois when I was still pretty young. And then he retired with disability, and went to work selling cars."

"My dad was a pilot during the Vietnam War," I said, wondering how ancient that sounded to these much-younger women. "He hangs out at the VFW, so most of his friends are fellow Air Force vets, but lots are younger than he is—closer to your dad in age, probably."

I was hoping to draw Janet out a little more but she just said, "Probably," shook out the child's pants she'd patched the knee of, and went to work on the other knee. I glanced at Natalie; she wasn't clearing her throat or glaring, so I tried, "Where are the rest of you from?"

"Originally New Hampshire," Emma said. "But Jason and I, Jason's my husband, we moved to Illinois, that's where—" She gestured at the group, glanced at Natalie, and finished, "That's where a lot of us are from."

"I'm from Indiana," Heather said.

Natalie didn't say anything but radiated faint disapproval.

I tried another angle. "How did you find your way to Pastor John's church?" One of the topics that would *usually* get an Evangelical Christian patient to loosen up was the story of their personal journey from "sinner" to "saved."

It worked, kind of: everyone perceptibly relaxed. "Oh,

Sister Emma and I met at a Rachel's Hope meeting years ago. Years and years."

"It's a biblical support group for women experiencing infertility," Emma said. "I'd had Bethany but hadn't been able to get pregnant again. This was before I had JJ."

"Pastor was preaching at a special service for women struggling with infertility and a group of us went together," Janet said. "He prayed over each of us and he told Sister Emma that God was going to open her womb and give her a son, and he told me that God had another plan for me."

"Did He?" I asked.

"Sister Emma got pregnant with JJ the next month," Janet said. "And he was right about me. Clearly God had other plans." Her brow furrowed a little. Emma reached over to squeeze Janet's hand.

"Anyway, that prayer service was pretty intense, and Pastor was preaching at a revival meeting the next week so we went to that," Emma said. "He talked about his vision of a community, a blessed community. I talked Jason into coming the next night, and the next. And Sister Janet brought her husband. Jason and I were churchgoers at the time, we went to Crossroads, but honestly we were pretty lukewarm. Pastor changed that."

Nods around the circle.

"So your kids," I said. "How old are they?"

"Bethany is thirteen now, and JJ is six."

I glanced out at the rest of the meeting hall. In the opposite corner I could see children around a few of the big tables, their heads bent over what I assumed was schoolwork. Emma leaned in to point. "Do you see the little ginger head and the green shirt? That's JJ. And Bethany's working in the kitchen today, but she's also a redhead."

"Does Jason have red hair?" Emma's hair was light brown with a little gray in it.

"He does," she said. "I compared him to Ron Weasley when we met—that was before I got saved, of course. I grew up secular." She and Janet exchanged a look and then she looked down at her sewing with a little bit of a smile.

Natalie started humming something, and everyone else joined in, singing a hymn in harmony as they stitched. I listened, wondering if the kids had access to books to learn to *read*—when I took a break from sewing to go use the bathroom a little while later, I sneaked a look at what they were working on. They were all doing math worksheets, so, hard to say.

Emma's daughter, Bethany, was washing her hands in the bathroom when I arrived—at least, that was my guess, given the hair. She had freckles and long red braids that made me think of Anne Shirley from *Anne of Green Gables.* When I came out of the bathroom, the younger kids were putting away their math worksheets and their teacher was herding them over to the entryway to put on boots and coats. Apparently it was recess time.

From the window by the sewing corner, I watched the younger children run outside. There was well-trampled snow in the center, deeper at the edges, and some of the kids had ventured into the deeper drifts to build a snow fort. A few boys were having a snowball fight.

"That's what I love the most about living here," Heather said, following my gaze. "It's the way childhood ought to be."

"What do you mean?" I asked.

"No screens," she said. "Back in the secular world, I didn't buy my kids phones or iPads but things like that were just *everywhere*. Anytime they played with a friend, even a Christian friend, they wound up on screens sooner or later. And I didn't feel like I could let them out of my sight, even just to play in the backyard. Here my kids can run all over. Real work—they start helping with chores almost as soon as they're walking, here—but real play, too."

"Which ones are yours?"

"The red hat and—oh, for crying out loud, he's not wearing his hat. The little boy in the blue coat, working on the snowman? I hope he left the hat inside and didn't *lose* it again. And that one, over there, the blond girl with the pigtails. Their older brother is working right now and their younger sister is napping in the crèche."

Back in the center of the room, Sarah rang a little brass bell for attention. "Women's fitness, fifteen minutes," she said.

There was a shift as people started putting away their tasks. Was this mandatory? Natalie settled back into her chair, so, apparently not. Emma, Janet, and Heather were all getting up. "Come join us," Emma suggested, and I trailed after her.

Tables were being rearranged again, and the rule of the hour seemed to be that men could not be present, because the handful of men and older boys who'd been in the community space all picked up and went elsewhere. I followed Emma and Grace into a room to the side that turned out to be a windowless storage room with shelves holding heathered gray sweat pants and T-shirts that looked like what I wore in my gym classes in the 1980s. I changed with everyone else, folded my clothes and put them on the shelf, and exited to find rows of worn yoga mats already laid out.

"I invite everyone"—was Sarah looking at me or beaming at everyone?—"to take a seat on their fitness mat in whatever posture works for you." She sat down, cross-legged. "We're going to start with silent prayer. Let's close our eyes. As we breathe in, we say silently: Lord Jesus, Son of God. As we breathe out we say: bless my work and make it holy."

I breathed in, thinking, *This feels like we're starting a yoga class.*

There was a faint click as Sarah started a tape. An actual cassette tape. (I peeked to be sure.) It played the same meandering synthesized music that routinely accompanied the yoga classes at my health club, although there I think they came out of the teacher's iPhone. And then Sarah invited us all to stand, and proceeded to lead us in a set of stretches and postures nearly identical to the ones I had done every time I'd let my friend Kim talk me into a yoga class.

Except instead of "downward-facing dog" it was "make a deep bow before the Lord" and instead of "upward-facing dog" it was "lift your face to the mountains," and instead of "warrior two" it was "leaning into the Lord," and instead of "corpse pose," of course, it was "Lazarus pose."

It was galling to hear the names, but a relief to go through the familiar exercises, to feel the stretch of the muscles around my hips, fatigue in my core and arms. I'd never stuck with yoga for more than a few months at a time, but sooner or later Kim always talked me into going back, and I always thought, *I should do this more regularly. Maybe this time I will.*

During "Lazarus pose," Sarah recited a prayer that presumably we were all supposed to be silently joining in on, thanking God for community, for strengthening our bodies, and for forgiving our sins. I wondered if she thought kidnapping me was a forgivable sin, or just not a sin at all.

"Bring your exercise clothes back here after you've showered and leave them in the laundry bag," Emma said, tapping a big sack. "It'll be lunchtime in fifteen minutes; there's just enough time to shower."

After lunch, I spent another hour sewing patches on children's pants, and then Emma invited me to "women's Bible study," which I went to in the hopes that I'd get a book out of the deal. Instead, the Bible was taken out from under lock and key by one of the men who then read a portion out loud to the women for discussion. The older girls were allowed to come, and I saw that I'd been right, the redheaded girl was Bethany, because she sat snuggled up with her mother.

The women discussed the story of Jonah, the guy who got eaten by the whale. They were focused on the idea that God's will was inescapable. Jonah tried to run; God found him. Jonah delivered his message but clearly *wanted* Nineveh to get destroyed; God spared it. Then they talked about how imperfect Jonah was, how his heart clearly wasn't in it when he did finally go to Nineveh, but despite this, the Ninevites repented and were saved.

"I have a question," Bethany said. She spoke in the same sweet, girlish voice as everyone else. It sounded less incongruous coming from an actual child.

"Yes?" said the older woman who'd led the Bible study.

"We're all here, in—in Tarshish." That's the town in the story that Jonah initially flees to. "We're in this wonderful, safe place, and everyone we used to know back in the world is out there ignorant of God's wrath. Not knowing their left hand from their right, like God says about the Ninevites. Why is it okay for us to live here?"

"Because we're *obeying* God by being here," the older woman said. "This is really a story about obedience, not a story about repentance. Jonah disobeys God, and God punishes him. Then he obeys God, and God uses his obedience. We're here because God spoke to Pastor, and we followed his leading. It may be that someday, we'll be sent out. But we should wait for the right time, for *God's* time. And for now, we're waiting here and doing our best to walk the path the Lord has made for us, as Pastor is showing us." She smiled at Bethany, a kind smile, not an angry one. "Does that make sense?"

"Oh, yes, Sister Caroline. Thank you."

I went back to the mending corner when Bible study was over, still without a book. Emma and Janet were still talking about Jonah. My mind drifted back to the yoga class, to the idea that they'd renamed *downward-facing dog*, for crying out loud. Christians didn't have anything against dogs. Well, maybe this cult did. I hadn't seen any dogs here. But probably they'd just wanted to rename *everything*, to remove the "taint" of this activity being yoga, which they probably thought was satanic or at least heathen.

It occurred to me that I'd never made it all the way through a yoga class without thinking about the charting I still had to do.

Of course, this time I had thought about escaping. I'd

thought, *I should come to the fitness class, build up my arm strength and core strength. I have no way to know what I might need to do to escape.*

Tonight's after-dinner ritual was "Testimonies and Confessions," and various people stepped up to deliver some sort of personal story, most of them pretty dull. Bethany rose to confess that she'd been tempted to shirk her work washing dishes today, but she'd prayed to God for strength and had overcome that temptation. I wondered if she'd been praying, or shirking, when I saw her in the bathroom.

The high drama came near the end, when one of the adult men confessed, weeping, to looking at pornography. He announced that he was putting himself in the hands of the Elders for discipline, and two men put their hands on his shoulders and guided him out.

The woman next to me, who had two young, somewhat squirmy kids, looked sort of contemptuous.

"What's going to happen to him?" I whispered.

"He'll get a thrashing."

"Wait, corporal punishment?"

"That's what 'putting yourself in the hands of the Elders' means. Or being put in the hands of the Elders, people don't always volunteer for it, but Turkey does a lot."

"Turkey?"

"That's his nickname. His real name's Toby."

"For porn? Or other stuff? Where does he even get porn?"

"Oh, he finds ways. Sometimes porn, sometimes impure thoughts."

I wondered if the adults here were so sheltered that none of them had the same thought I did, that possibly Toby's "impure thoughts" involved a sexual fetish for the sort of punishment he was volunteering for. But if he had "found ways" to look at porn, did that mean he had a hidden phone? Maybe they *all* had phones tucked away. Maybe I could find one.

THE WORD *OBSTETRICS* COMES from the Latin word *obstetrix*, which means midwife. Literally it means "stands opposite to," and references the person who stands opposite to the woman giving birth. (Although, hilariously, the same root word turned into *obstacle*, and I once had a grumpy patient who pointed this out. She was not having a good time that day, although we managed to avoid a C-section and she went home with a healthy baby.)

When I did my residency, back in the mists of time (by which I mean the late 1990s), one of the attending physicians who trained me was a white-haired older doctor who'd seen a whole range of birthing practices come and go. He liked to tell residents that obstetrics was the science of waiting. Most of the time, if you just wait for the cervix and uterus to do their jobs, things go better than they would if you put your oar in. You need to pay attention, because sometimes your skills are needed very suddenly, but he believed that the most critical skill for a good obstetrician was patience. The ability to just stand opposite to, no more and no less.

I was actually pretty good at waiting when a patient was in labor. But there was a difference between saying things to patients like "I'm not really the one in charge here, the baby is" and *really, truly not being the one in charge here.* Waiting for a chance to escape was a completely different sort of patience, and not something I felt particularly skilled at.

In *The Onyx Dagger*, the escape was assisted by a telepathic cat, but still required patience because he was not initially a friendly cat. You could usually recognize a telepathic cat in the world of the book because they had heterochromatic eyes; the cat Deirdre spotted was missing an eye, so she couldn't be sure, and he was feral and wouldn't come within touching distance. She'd saved morsels of food to tempt him, and he had come closer, finally rubbing against her offered hand. The physical contact let her confirm her guess.

The cat had to *fully trust her* before she could look out through the cat's eyes and know when the guards were distracted, asleep, or gone, though, and that took days; they were being marched toward the mines, so there was a deadline, and she couldn't let herself push things with the cat too quickly or the cat would run away. The chance had come at nearly the last possible moment; the cat had not only allowed Deirdre to look through his eyes but had taken suggestions for things that would create a distraction, which was good because logically the guards would only get *more* vigilant as they got closer to the mines and their prisoners would be more desperate to escape.

The cat had a name, in the book, but it was one of those names with lots of consonants and no vowels—Rrrtrxrl or something like that—and I couldn't remember it. Back in the pre-audiobook era, you could have a name that was just fully unpronounceable. Reading the book, I'd called him Retrixeral in my head, but that was definitely not correct.

I dropped off that night thinking about Retrixeral and had another nightmare, but at least this time it was your garden-variety obstetrician's nightmare: I was in a casino and someone had gotten a jackpot with a slot machine, and now babies were shooting out and I was trying to catch them and dropping them. I woke up filled with anxiety and then thought about the dream and laughed with relief. *A slot machine full of newborn babies, ridiculous.* I rolled over and thought about cats again until I'd dropped back off.

CHAPTER 4

SATURDAY WAS A CLINIC day, but a different sort of clinic day: instead of examining pregnant women, we mostly examined children.

I am not a pediatrician. Obstetricians obviously get to see a lot of babies, and a certain number of older children, but we are not the ones *responsible* for babies once they're separated from their mothers. If you have me look into a toddler's ear with an otoscope, I can tell you if it's infected, of course, but I have no skill in getting wiggly little kids to hold still long enough that I can have a look. Nor do I know much about the normal development of children. But I didn't want to imply that I thought they ought to go kidnap themselves a pediatrician, so I examined the children and did the best I could at identifying problems that needed some sort of intervention.

It was not surprising that a cult that beat adults also routinely physically punished children. One of the boys, a little freckled guy with a spiky blond buzz cut, had multiple welts, some half healed and some fresh. I couldn't tell what he'd been hit with. He was otherwise healthy, and his sister, a toddler, didn't have any contusions that didn't look like the result of normal tumbles. His mother looked exhausted in a way that parenting young children didn't explain.

I thought about my pediatrician friend Lori, and whether she'd ever given me advice that fit this particular situation. Pediatricians were trained to screen mothers for postnatal depression; surely they also at least referred mothers who were clearly unhealthy in other ways. "I'm worried about you," I said, bluntly. "Are you getting enough sleep?"

"Probably not," she said, and forced out a laugh.

"Have you had your iron levels checked? Thyroid levels?"

"If you want to draw her blood, we can send it out to a lab," Sarah said.

"No—" The woman pulled back. "I thought this was just to look at Andrew and Missy." She looked at Sarah. "I don't like needles."

"But—"

"Oh, someone else is here, I hear them coming," she said, gathering up her children.

No one was there. "I really think she's not well," I said.

"I'll ask Pastor John to ask her husband to send her here for a checkup," Sarah said.

I also thought that her discipline methods, such as

they were, clearly weren't working, if she was having to beat a six-year-old that hard, that often. I was afraid to say that out loud for fear this would be taken to mean *perhaps you should hit him harder.*

The next arrival was Bethany, escorting her brother, JJ.

"You've just about outgrown the children's appointments, haven't you?" Sarah said, warmly, as the two children sat down. "When's your birthday, Bethany?"

"Not until March, Sister Sarah," Bethany said politely.

I examined JJ, then Bethany. Both were mostly healthy, but Bethany needed glasses and a dental filling.

To my relief, Sarah did not make any noises about having me try to drill the tooth. "How nearsighted do you think she is?"

"Very," I said.

"Can you write her an eye prescription?"

"Absolutely not," I said. "I don't have the equipment to determine her glasses prescription, and I wouldn't know how to use the equipment if I had it. She probably doesn't need an ophthalmologist, she probably just needs an optometrist, but someone's going to have to take her to a town."

"Hmm." Sarah made a face. "That's not how we do things." She sent a runner to fetch all the adults in the cult with glasses, and had Bethany try on each pair and say if they were better or worse. One of the men's pairs of glasses seemed to provide her with pretty decent focus, and he was instructed to go get a copy of his prescription so they could order a pair of glasses for Bethany that matched.

"How does the tooth feel, Bethany?" Sarah asked her. "Any pain?"

"No pain, Sister Sarah."

"Pray on it, swish with fluoride morning and night, and let us know if it does start hurting."

As the door closed behind Bethany's red pigtails, I asked, ". . . And if it does start hurting?"

"We have a set of forceps and Brother Joshua pulls it. Oh, don't look so shocked! You know we have nitrous oxide."

"That seems so unnecessary when you could just take her to a dentist now, and get it filled."

"That's not how we do things," she said again.

We seemed to be done seeing kids for a bit: Sarah was busying herself counting sheets and towels in the cupboard and making a list of things she needed from the laundry. "Why are there no books here?" I asked. "Does 'how you do things' mean no reading?"

"What?" She turned around, her eyes a little bright. "We have books."

"Can I have a book, then?"

There was a long pause, and then Sarah said, "Pastor had a revelation from God last year that we should set aside worldly distractions, as a community. There was a discernment committee, and after a lot of prayer they decided that we would set aside all the books, bringing out just what is necessary. What is *most* necessary. And that would help us to see which books are needed, and which are a distraction."

"And Bibles for individual reading were worldly distractions?"

"In Christ's day, most people would not have been able to read the Bible to themselves. They'd have listened to someone else read it. Having a single Bible that we treat as a treasure makes it feel more special, helps us pay attention to every precious word. The way water tastes incredible when you're really, really thirsty."

"So are the children not learning to read?"

"Of course the children are learning to read. The reading instruction books are necessary; they're brought out for lessons."

"I didn't see any on Friday."

"Friday is a math-work day."

This was an *absolutely terrible* way to teach children to read. "How long ago did all the books get put away?" I asked.

"It's February now, the revelation was in May, so . . . ten months." Sarah swallowed and I saw her jaw muscles tighten. "It was a sacrifice, for me personally. But we are called to do hard things, and it turns out novels really were a distraction."

I nodded. "What sort of books did you like to read?" I asked.

"Anything. Historical fiction was my favorite. Before I got saved, I mean. We had . . . Before we put away all the books, we put away fiction. I had been reading biographies because those are sometimes . . . those are basically just as good."

"Who were you reading about in May? I mean, before Pastor John's revelation about putting away *all* the books."

"Clara Barton," she said. "Founder of the Red Cross."

"Did you ever read *The Hiding Place*?" I asked, more because I thought the answer was *yes* than because I'd particularly loved the book. That was a memoir by a Dutch woman and Evangelical Christian who'd hidden Jews during the Holocaust.

I saw the spark of recognition in her eyes. "I loved that book."

"I read it years ago," I said. "I remember it was really good." I had read it in high school and I remembered liking it at the time, but I hadn't revisited it in part because I was pretty sure it would not have aged well. I'd reread it now, if I could.

There was a knock at the door—another young mother shepherding in several children. I wondered what they'd do if I announced that someone had cancer, decided I'd save that tactic for another day, and turned to smile at the mother.

Sarah was right about the deprivation making text feel precious, I thought that night as I read the ingredients on my toothpaste tube while brushing my teeth. As a child, I'd read the nutrition facts on the cereal box in the morning while eating. I would read an entire library of cereal boxes now, if I could. I'd read drug package inserts, if I had any. I'd read a licensing agreement for a phone app. A Bible consisting only of the listings of "begats." It felt almost like a hunger. There was steam on the mirror when I took my shower before bed: I wrote *courage* in the steam, and looked at the word for a long time.

That night in bed, instead of *The Onyx Dagger*, I thought about Corrie ten Boom and *The Hiding Place*. She'd been caught, eventually—the Jews she'd sheltered successfully hid and remained safe, but Corrie spent months in prison and was then sent to a concentration camp. In prison, she'd struggled with boredom to the point of treasuring visits from ants, which she'd observed with close interest. Eventually someone slipped her a Bible, and she talked about how now she had *the word of God with her* and—not to question Corrie's framing or anything, but while reading her memoir as a teen, I absolutely assumed that part of her joy in that moment was just about having something to read.

Corrie had spent her time in the concentration camp forgiving and periodically ministering to the Nazis who imprisoned her. I tried to imagine spending my time here spreading understanding of the scientific method to the children. *Let me tell you the good news about evolution and natural selection.* That would sure be playing the long game. I closed my eyes and imagined myself instead in the vine-covered treehouse where Deirdre brought Isabelle for sanctuary after rescuing her. *Where are we?* Isabelle had asked. *This is beautiful, can we stay here forever?*

We can't stay here forever because danger will follow us, Deirdre had said, stroking Isabelle's hair. *We can stay here a moment, though. Let us treasure the joys of this moment.*

I WOKE UP HOT and sweaty. There was something deeply unfair about the fact that I was still having hot flashes while kidnapped. I shoved my blankets off, put my shoes on, and went outside the cabin just to cool down.

My exterior light clicked on. It was snowing: I looked up at the flakes spinning down, glittering bright in the light. I couldn't tell what time it was, just that it was still very much night.

Some young man—not Brother Ethan tonight, someone else—came right over to check on me. "Do you need anything?" he asked.

"Just to cool off," I said. "I'm having a hot flash."

"Oh," he said, and backed away like it might be contagious. "I'll leave you to it, then."

I stifled a snort. I should start coming out every night, every time I woke up to pee, and tell them all it was hot flashes. Eventually, "Dr. Liz comes out at night due to hot flashes" would become the sort of thing they just accepted, and they'd stop checking on me. I could walk right out and they wouldn't notice.

The heat was fading, replaced with a chill. I went back inside, kicked off my shoes again, and got a drink of water. My pajamas were damp from my sweat, so I dug through the drawers looking for something to change into. They hadn't given me extra pajamas, so I put on some of the scrubs and went back to bed. I found myself fuming, thinking about the lack of extra pajamas. If I knew where Sarah slept, I could go bang on her door and tell her I needed something dry to sleep in. Well, or I could tell the patrolling young man with a gun that I needed fresh pajamas—he'd be mortified, too, which made it almost ideal. Getting back up felt like a lot of effort, though.

When I woke up properly, there'd been some real snow accumulation. Someone had put a plow attachment on this little rugged golf cart thing and was clearing the walkway from the houses up to the meeting house, although I could see trails people had made wading through the knee-deep snow ahead of the plow. I made my way up to the building.

"I need more than one pair of pajamas," I said to Sarah by way of greeting. "I have hot flashes at night and I need to be able to change."

She looked taken aback. "Of course," she said. "I'll let

Sister Kate know. Are you on any medication for it? Because we can—"

"I'm not on any medication for it," I growled. "I just need to be able to *put on fresh pajamas* if I sweat through the first pair at night. Fresh sheets, too."

"I'll put down that you should get air-conditioning, come summer," she said kindly, and I only barely managed to hide my full-body flinch at the idea that I might still be here in June.

The cult had scripture reading and prayer of some kind every day after dinner, and Sunday was *all-day* church. After breakfast there was an hour of "worship music," which featured Emma singing and a band that included Brother Ethan with an electric guitar. Then a room divider got pulled across the room so that the adults could have "church" and the children could have "children's church," which would have worked better as a division with something more soundproof than a room divider. I was sent to children's church, which seemed to be the kids under ten, with about half the teenage girls there to try to keep them in line. I wasn't sure if I was there in my capacity as an ignorant child who needed basic instruction, or in my capacity as a girl capable of babysitting.

Joy was in charge of children's church. As we heard Pastor John's voice (muffled, because he was speaking with his back to the partition and the speakers faced away from us), Joy led the kids in more songs and then had the kids go around with prayer requests. Bethany requested prayers that her dental cavity heal itself so she didn't need her tooth pulled. I winced at that, especially since she sounded absolutely sincere.

She was followed by a girl who looked about nine who

somewhat petulantly prayed that her brother would remember to wipe his feet when he came inside later because she didn't want to have to mop the floor *again*. "Constance," Joy said, reprovingly. "Use your gentle voice." Constance's face darkened and Joy reached across the table to tap her chin. "The Lord's rules are sweeter than honey," she said. "Take a deep breath and we'll let you try again in a minute."

JJ, Bethany's little brother, asked for prayers for his mother because he'd heard her crying the other day. Another boy wanted to pray that we had garlic bread with the lasagna this week. That set off more meal-related prayers—someone wanted to pray for dessert to come every night. A girl who looked like she was right on the line between "child there to be taught" and "teenager present to provide the babysitting" prayed for unspecified wisdom, which turned out to be the default thing you said if you couldn't think of anything better.

We circled back to Constance. She had smoothed out the fury in her face, put on what sounded to me like an obviously false happy tone, and prayed for God to make her more patient with her brother.

"Much better," Joy said. She turned to me. "Dr. Liz? What would you like for us to pray for?"

I almost had them pray for my father, who was probably very worried by now, or would be soon when I didn't return his Sunday afternoon phone call. But other than Joy, these were children. If I persuaded someone like Bethany of the rightness of my position that they should let me go, the most likely result was going to be Bethany getting into trouble. "Wisdom," I said.

Joy asked everyone to pray for a safe delivery for her

baby. Then she glanced over her shoulder towards the room divider, and sighed. On the other side of the partition, we could hear Pastor John's voice, though not his words; he was still on the upswing of a crescendo, and clearly not getting done for a while. "I'll tell you all a story," she said. "Which story would you like?"

"Can we hear Cinderella?" asked one of the little girls near the front.

Joy shook her head. "It's Sunday. You can have a Bible story."

"Baby Moses!" one of the other girls said.

Joy started the story of Baby Moses in the bullrushes with "once upon a time . . ." like she was telling a fairy tale, and I was pretty sure she made some mistakes, although since neither of us had a Bible it wasn't like I could check. From Pharaoh's daughter rescuing Moses from the Nile, she went on to a fairly detailed story about child-Moses and his friend, the son of the pharaoh, that was absolutely not in the Bible and I realized after about ten minutes (it was a long story) was a retelling of portions of *Tom Sawyer*, with the pharaoh's son in the role of Tom and Moses as Huck Finn.

When the adults finally came to get the children for lunch, I had a moment with Joy and said, "Can't wait for the sequel where Moses takes a raft down the Mississippi."

She glanced at me and shrugged. "Sure was easier back when I could read them chapters of books."

The snow had continued to fall throughout the morning, and in the afternoon, as most of the adults went back for more church, the children were allowed to bundle up and go out to play in the fresh snow. Joy went in to sit with the adults for the afternoon worship service, and a few of the other women came out to supervise the children, with the help of a couple of the teenage boys. I was left with the children again, and mostly stood and watched as snowflakes drifted down and melted on me. The teenage boys ran around and played with the younger kids, helping them build a new snow fort, throw snowballs, and make snow angels. Early in the afternoon, two of the boys were pretending to be Spider-Man and the Hulk; one of the teenage boys redirected them into pretending to defend the cattle herd from a wolf pack, but as soon as the older boys moved on, the younger kids went back to playing Spider-Man. The boy playing the Hulk was Andrew, the little blond boy I'd noticed at the clinic. The one with the sick mother. And the extensive welts from being beaten.

As the afternoon wore on and the snow tapered off, several of the men came out with shovels to manually clear the narrower walkways while someone else plowed with the golf cart again. People were coming out of the community building to round up their children and get them into dry clothes before dinner. The band, now including Joy, was playing a last song for the people preparing the meal.

In the snow, with the sun setting and lamps glowing through the curtains over the windows, and small children in heavy coats skipping home ahead of their mothers, the compound looked picturesque. It looked like a village scene in a painting. For a moment, I saw it as I thought Emma probably saw it: welcoming, peaceful, intimate. An idyllic place to be a child.

"Do *you* know any stories, Dr. Elizabeth?" a voice asked. It was Bethany, standing at my elbow.

"Oh, yes," I said. "Would you like to hear one?"

A hesitation, and the light in her face dimmed a fraction. "I shouldn't ask for a story Pastor wouldn't like for you to tell," she said. "That wouldn't be good for me."

"Did you like reading, when there were books?"

She sighed. "I think it might have been my fault Pastor decided they were a distraction," she confessed in a low voice. "I used to sneak off to read instead of doing my work. It was right after I got another thrashing for it that Pastor decided *all* the books had to be put away. And I think he was right. I'd read anything right now, if I could. Even *The Blossoms of Morality*, if that's all I had."

"Do you ever pray that God will send Pastor a new revelation and give everyone their books back?"

She leaned in and whispered, "Praying for things against Pastor's will isn't a good idea."

I was going to ask her about her favorite book when she pulled away. "I'm supposed to be setting the tables," she gasped, and darted back inside.

The compound was now in deep twilight. I walked down to my house to put on dry clothes before dinner. I opened the door and then recoiled with a gasp: the light was on, and Pastor John was standing inside.

"Come in, Dr. Elizabeth," he said.

I glanced over my shoulder; two of the men were lurking down on the path between the houses. I hadn't noticed anyone following me, and they weren't moving any closer, they were just there. I went in.

"All the way in," Pastor John added. "Shut the door, don't let the heat out."

I closed the door and leaned against it.

Pastor John was sitting on my bed, which had been

pulled out from the wall. The hash marks I'd made to track days were visible, and the pen I'd stuffed under my mattress was in his hand.

I felt myself starting to shake, wondering if I'd be beaten, or worse.

"I came by to see how you were settling in," Pastor John said. "How would you say you're settling in, Doctor?"

The question hung in the air. He was waiting for an answer.

"I—you *kidnapped* me."

"We *rescued* you," he said, gravely. "The Tribulation is underway—body and soul, you were forfeit to Satan's minions, for your past sins. But as it transpired, you were chosen. Chosen by God to live in the haven among the righteous, blessed to deliver the blessed children."

I reject everything you're saying warred with *I need to cooperate*. I said nothing, and lowered my eyes.

"Now." He stood. I couldn't back away from him; my back was already against my door. "Clean those up." He pulled a rag out of his pocket and pointed at the marks, like I was a child who'd drawn on the wall. I went to the bathroom and wet the rag, came out and cleaned them away. When the last trace of the marks was gone, he said, "I understand why you feel you need to know the date; you're a doctor. Your *job* is to know whether it's time for a baby to come yet, or not. So I have brought you a calendar." He set down a tiny month-by-month desk calendar, along with a blue gel-ink pen with a cap. "Today is circled."

He paused, expectantly, and it took me a couple of seconds to realize what he was waiting for.

"Thank you," I said.

"You're welcome. Don't draw on the walls again. No dinner for you tonight." He paused on his way out, looked back, and said, "No one *wants* you to get a thrashing, Doctor." He closed the door behind him, and I sat down on the bed, shaking.

CHAPTER 5

WEEKS PASSED.

Every morning I drew an X through the date on my calendar. Every night, I told myself some fragment of *The Onyx Dagger*. I visualized the yellowed pages of my paperback copy, the one I'd read over and over as a teen, that I'd been too sentimental to throw away even once I had a less battered copy. There was a splash of tea on the corner of the page where they first met the dragon. A badly creased page where Isabelle comes back to herself, finally, after her rescue. Blue ballpoint pen where I'd underlined *there must be a way*.

On Mondays, I was told I'd be seeing women for prenatal and postnatal care, but since nearly every adult woman on the compound was pregnant, trying to become pregnant, or recently pregnant, that encompassed a lot. My first week, in addition to checking postnatal women for healing, I gave a pregnant woman fluconazole for a yeast infection and drained another woman's massive, painful Bartholin's cyst while reassuring her that these were something that could just happen. A lot of women wonder if they're something sexually transmitted. (And, they *can* be caused by STDs, but most of the time they aren't.)

Again, despite the fact that these women seemed to be entirely on board with a kidnapped doctor, in the moments that I was providing them with care, I found myself unable to do less than my best for any of them, just as back in Minot I'd sometimes stayed up past midnight doing charting, even when I knew I'd have to be up at six. At least charting here was just a matter of Sarah jotting down in a notebook that it was Sister Brianna who had the cyst I'd drained, and I'd told her to use a sitz bath at least twice a day, and that she couldn't have sex for a while. She seemed very uncertain about that instruction, and I looked at Sarah. "She really *cannot* have sex until she's healed," I said. "This isn't going to heal otherwise." Sarah said she would talk to Pastor John and have him talk to Brianna's husband.

My youngest patient that morning was a newlywed who was there because after six months of marriage she wasn't yet pregnant. Sarah called the girl Sister Chloe, but tripped up a few times because apparently you were only "Sister Firstname" here once you were married, and this girl had been just "Chloe" not all that long ago.

After a couple of questions got me barely audible, entirely mumbled answers, I took Sarah aside and told her that if she wanted me to chase down the explanation for Chloe's infertility she was going to *have* to leave me alone with this girl. Or I could leave her alone with Sarah. Explaining what was going on to *two* women was clearly going to be too stressful.

"I've tried to get a straight answer out of her twice already," Sarah muttered.

"Guess it's on me, then," I said. "Go take a walk."

To my surprise, Sarah *did* take a walk, and I briefly wondered if I could appeal to Chloe to help me get out of here. Looking at her wide, fearful eyes, I decided that the answer was *no*. Probably better to keep this conversation focused; maybe that could help me lull Sarah into trusting me alone with more people.

"Tell me about what happens when you have sex with your husband," I said.

"It's not like I expected," she whispered.

There's a story that circulates about a couple that spends years trying to get pregnant, only to see a doctor who realizes they've been having anal sex the whole time. This is almost certainly an urban legend, and I briefly wondered if I was about to have that story come true, but Chloe instead haltingly explained that her husband penetrated her—vaginally—but for a minute or less. It didn't sound like he was ejaculating.

This sounded like sexual dysfunction and not like actual infertility. "I think I need to see your husband," I said. "It sounds like he's the one who needs my advice."

Just before leaving, Chloe took a deep breath and said, "If God doesn't bless us with a child soon, I'm afraid—Nick is a good man. I don't want Pastor to give me to anyone else. I want Nick."

"Are you saying that you'll be forced to divorce if you don't get pregnant?"

"Oh, no, God hates divorce."

"What's going to happen if you don't get pregnant?"

"Brother Ethan's got no wife right now, and Pastor might decide I should take Brother Ethan's wife's place."

"God hates divorce, but swapping around a bride because she didn't get pregnant is allowed?"

"Well, God did command us to be fruitful," she said.

"What about Janet?" I said. "I thought Sister Janet was infertile."

"Yes, ma'am," she said.

I gave up trying to understand this. "Send Nick—Brother Nick to me," I said. "Tell him I want to see him."

Also on Mondays, Emma and Jason took the van (the same one I'd been kidnapped with) and went out for a several-hours-long trip to grocery shop. They came home with coolers and bags of food in Walmart grocery sacks, which I sometimes saw people unloading in the afternoon. In "school," the children worked on reading; the books were unlocked and dutifully passed out, and even the fluent readers were allowed a few hours with a book. I was briefly tempted to try to filch one away, but then I found out it was Bethany who had to gather them up before lunch, count them, and lock them away again, and it was Bethany who'd take the blame if there was a shortfall in the number. Bethany, I also noticed, did not get reading time with a book—it looked like it was just the grade-school-aged kids who got to read.

On Tuesdays, I saw Harvest residents (I called them *Harvesters* in my head, like the agricultural equipment, but they referred to themselves as "the Blessed") who wanted to see a doctor for some reason other than pregnancy. Jason came in the first week because he'd been having pain in one of his knees. I thought it was probably a meniscal tear; we got out the ultrasound machine and I did my best but couldn't spot it. Of course, I'm not an orthopedist. I'm also not a physical therapist, and he would probably benefit from physical therapy. Sarah had already looked up some exercises for knee pain, which she hinted that he probably wasn't doing, and she printed them off again and sent him on his way.

"It might still be a meniscal tear," I said.

"I didn't see one, either," she said, dismissively. "Some men are just malingerers. You should see Brother Jason with a cold."

Chloe's husband Nick came in on a Tuesday two weeks after I'd seen Chloe. Sarah's willingness to leave me alone with Chloe turned out to be heavily predicated on Chloe's extreme timidity. She refused to leave me alone with Nick, saying it was inappropriate for a woman to be alone with a man not her husband under any circumstances. I suggested that Chloe be brought in to supervise me with her husband; Sarah refused to go along with that, either. I could talk to Nick, but she needed to be present for it.

Nick was young, like Chloe, and quiet, like Chloe. I could easily understand why Chloe didn't want to trade him for Brother Ethan, who I thought would probably give me the creeps even if I had not heard that he'd committed a murder. Chloe and Nick were both the children of high-status older men, "Elders" who I didn't know particularly well, and apparently Chloe had *asked* for Nick, which was apparently part of why this relationship was viewed with so much suspicion.

I asked Sarah to please at least sit at the far end of the room and pretend to be working on something else, which she did. "Good morning, Brother Nick," I said, having him sit down opposite me on the rolling chair. "I'm Dr. Elizabeth, and I asked Sister Chloe to send you in because it sounded like you might be having some difficulties getting her in a family way."

He nodded, silently, and stared at the floor.

"Can you tell me, do you need . . . better instructions? An explanation of what to do?"

He shook his head. "Brother Jason talked to me before the wedding," he said.

"Are you having trouble maintaining an erection?"

He looked at me, wide-eyed, and said, "I shouldn't be having trouble. Chloe's beautiful, anyone can see that. She's a beautiful girl."

I looked at his bright, terrified eyes, his absolutely rigid shoulders, and his hands clasping each other in his lap, and I thought, *This poor boy.*

I had a couple of guesses as to what the actual problem was, and at the very top of my list was that Brother Nick was gay. The way he said, "Chloe's beautiful, anyone can see that" had the ring of someone trying to convince himself that *beautiful* also meant *desirable*. While some deeply closeted gay men in this community might overcompensate with bluster and aggression, Nick was merely himself, gentle and quiet. I could understand why Chloe wanted to keep him.

"A girl can be perfectly beautiful and entirely desirable

and there are a long list of reasons why a man might have trouble maintaining an erection that have nothing to do with his desire for her," I said. Even if Sarah hadn't been here, asking Nick if he was maybe just not that into girls seemed like a bad approach. "I'm going to send you home today with some sildenafil, which you may have heard of under the brand name Viagra." We had it in the cabinet; Sarah gave it to several of the older men.

"Isn't that for old dudes?" Nick said.

"Lots of older men take it," I said. "But it works for anyone dealing with erectile dysfunction. My theory is that you're in sort of an anxiety loop, and giving you a medication that will just fully guarantee an erection will help you have some procreative intercourse. I've seen"—this was true—"quite a few men for whom that worked." I mean, I was not the main person who treated them, since I'm an ob-gyn, but I see men in my office pretty regularly when they come with their wives for prenatal appointments, and I'd heard all sorts of stories. "Are you able to climax from masturbation?"

He drew back, horrified. "I don't do *that*."

I decided to stick with the sildenafil option for now, rather than bringing up the possibility of artificial insemination. "I can give Chloe some tests that will tell her when her most fertile time is; take one pill, wait a half hour, and then try. Use some lubricant to ease the way so you won't hurt Chloe, and if you have to stroke yourself a bit before you enter her, as long as you reach climax while penetrating her, you'll be able to get her pregnant."

I fetched the key from Sarah, unlocked the cabinet, and got out the pill packets, having him list the meds he was currently taking (absolutely nothing, not even a multivitamin) and running through the risk factors (he didn't have any). He stared frozen in the chair for a moment, staring at the little boxes of pills.

"Is there anything else I can help you with?" I asked.

His eyes were still bright with a little bit of terror. "Sister Ginny, she was Chloe's sister. Older sister."

"That was Brother Ethan's wife, the one who died?"

"Yeah. She was a lot like Chloe. Beautiful and quiet and you feel like a little wind might blow her away, you know? And when she had her baby, she *died*."

Oh. I mean, I might still be right about him being gay, but that wasn't the real problem.

"Brother Nick," I said, very firmly, "I will not let Sister Chloe die. Not from pregnancy, not from childbirth."

I could see some of the tension going out of his shoulders, his ears flushing red. He nodded once, then gathered up his things, including the pills, put on his coat, and went back out into the snow.

"I gave him those pills a month and a half ago," Sarah said, the second the door had closed. "I don't think he's *using* them."

"Maybe he will now," I said. "What did kill Ginny?"

Sarah's face looked shuttered. "Severe placental abruption at thirty-six weeks."

Placental abruption is when the placenta detaches early from the uterine wall. This can happen spontaneously or be the result of trauma. With the severe kind, where immediate delivery is necessary, if you get the mother to a hospital quickly, an emergency cesarean usually makes it a scary story, not a tragic one.

"The other doctor was here?" I asked.

"Dr. Jana, yes. She said we should call an ambulance and that there wasn't anything she could do."

"What did you do?"

"I gave her Pitocin," she said. "I couldn't do a C-section, I wouldn't know how, but I thought maybe if I could speed things up it would save them, or at least save Ginny. It didn't."

Pitocin would be useless in that situation. I'd never lost a mother to placental abruption. I tried to imagine standing there, *not acting*, a woman bleeding out in front of me. I would absolutely not be able to do that.

"Sister Ginny was so young," Sarah said. "It broke everyone's heart, losing her."

"How young was she?"

"Seventeen."

I blinked. Ginny had been Chloe's *older* sister. "How old is Chloe?"

"Fifteen." Sarah tilted her head to the side. "Pastor believes that it's better to marry young."

"How old is Nick?"

"He's eighteen."

I was aghast and trying to hide it, but I could tell from Sarah's face that my reaction was leaking through, no matter how hard I was trying to feign neutrality. "Why does Pastor John say it's better to marry young? Help me understand." *I need to understand enough that I can keep from radiating horror at these poor girls who are depending on me.*

"Sex drives are strong in teens—I know, you just saw Nick, he's hardly a good illustration of that point, but it's good for the teenage boys to know they'll be able to marry soon! Fertility is high in the young, so they'll be able to have more children. Teenagers live up to the expectations placed upon them; if we treat them as adults, they act more like adults. Godly marriages know no age."

"Isn't Joy twenty? How long ago did she marry?"

"Oh, Joy married a little later. She was keeping house for her daddy, you see. He wasn't ready to let her move out until he'd remarried."

I nodded, trying to stuff my horror deep inside. "For my 'continuing education' today," I said, "I'd like you to go over what happened with Sister Ginny, in detail."

I did "continuing education" on Tuesdays; I had found it cloying when Sarah called it that the first week, but I had, in fact, learned a few new things. For example, how to use nitrous oxide in deliveries. I'd suggested twice that if they ordered me some medical textbooks, I could brush up on orthopedics. (Not that *Surgical Exposures in Orthopedics* would be relaxing recreational reading. It was more my equivalent of Bethany's *Blossoms of Morality.*) Sarah had said she would consider talking to Pastor John and made it clear, mainly through vibes, that I should not hold my breath. In any case, hearing all the details of exactly what happened with Ginny would be useful ahead of future emergencies.

I'd heard that Tuesdays were "feed delivery" for the ranch. They had a small herd of cattle, which I'd seen only from a distance, but they also had a barn full of chickens, and chickens need grain, at least if you're raising them at scale. "Delivery" made me think that maybe, *maybe* an outsider would be coming to the ranch, but no: Brandon (the same Brandon who helped kidnap me) took a pickup truck from the locked building and drove it somewhere, returning in late afternoon with a load of feed for the chickens and anything else people had told him to pick up in town. At the school, the children all got lectures on "history" and "science" from one of the men. He got a book, but the kids didn't.

On Wednesday mornings, I did prenatal and postnatal care. The women here were, at least, getting more attentive prenatal care than most of my patients on the outside. The children doing beginner literacy did reading again; all the other children did math. In the afternoon, all the women and children went to the dining hall for what they called "Marketplace Day."

The cult talked a lot about their goal of full self-sufficiency, but as the feed delivery and grocery shopping trips demonstrated, they were not at all close to that goal yet. They brought in income by selling things online. In addition to the hand-beaded veils and other custom clothing items, they had an Etsy store that sold handmade wood toys. A couple of the men worked on cutting, shaping, and assembling little wood trucks and trains. The most time-consuming and least skill-intensive part of making nice wood toys was the sanding: that's what they had the rest of us do.

They set us up in a rudimentary assembly line, with the tables at one end working with coarse-grained sanding pads, the tables at the far end using polishing cloths. On my first week, I dutifully sanded the open-grained red-oak blocks I was handed, thinking about my father and how quickly the need for endless sanding had killed my desire to learn to do woodworking from him. Near the end of the afternoon I asked Sister Samantha, who I'd seen in the morning because she was four months pregnant and the mother of three already, whether there was a reason they didn't have dust masks for us.

"Well, the men wear them while power sanding, of course," she said. "But we're just hand sanding."

"It's still a lot of dust," I said. "It's not actually good for us. We should be wearing dust masks to protect our lungs."

"Oh. Maybe someone should say something to Pastor."

I wondered if this was going to require a full-scale "you kidnapped yourselves a doctor, maybe you should listen to your doctor" fit, but the following week there were optional dust masks and after seeing me put one on, so did about half the other women.

Thursdays, I saw pregnant women in the morning. The children all did math, followed by one hour of reading practice, during which the older children were only allowed to read the Bible.

Thursday afternoon, I saw anyone else in Harvest who wanted to see a doctor. My second week I found out the kids spent their Thursday afternoons on "life instruction," which generally meant farm chores for the boys and cooking and other household-type chores for the girls, because a teenage boy got brought in in the throes of an asthma attack.

"He needs albuterol," I said. "Do you have albuterol?" Sarah unlocked the medications and I explained to him how to use the inhaler. "What triggered this?" I asked him.

"I don't know," he said.

"What were you doing when you started having trouble breathing?"

"Cleaning the chicken barn," he said. "We were doing life instruction and the boys my age work with the chickens."

I turned to Sarah. "He's probably allergic to something in the barn. Chicken feathers, maybe. He needs to *not* clean the chicken barn."

"I can advise his mother, she can talk to his father, and his father can bring your concern to Pastor. But he's twelve, and the twelve-year-old boys clean the chicken barn as part of life instruction."

"Did he just—" I turned to the boy. "Did you just turn twelve?"

"Yes, ma'am. Yes, Doctor. On Monday."

"Have you had asthma attacks before?"

"I get wheezy sometimes, but not like this."

"Tell Pastor John that if he wants this boy to turn thirteen he should find him some job that isn't the chicken barn, and young man, if you're going into the chicken barn you need to at least wear a high-grade filter mask like an N95 the whole time you're in there. Not just a dust mask like we wore sanding earlier this week, a *filter mask*."

"The inhaler helped a lot," he said.

"If you overuse an inhaler it will stop working. Keep that in your pocket in case you need it, but you can't just expose yourself to a major allergen that triggers a reaction and rely on your inhaler to save you, because one day it *won't*."

Later that same day, I saw someone who'd gotten a "thrashing"—not Turkey, someone else. It was one of the adult women, not pregnant, who'd been hit with a narrow implement like a switch on her thighs and buttocks hard enough to draw blood. One of her wounds was oozing and she was concerned—reasonably enough—about infection. She'd started using a topical antibiotic but only in the last day; I gave her a stronger one and told her to come right back if it got any worse.

Back in my real life, when adult patients came in with marks like this, it was usually from consensual BDSM activities. Children with marks from beatings merited an automatic call to CPS; adults required some sort of conversation. Women who had them consensually were always relieved that I, a respectable middle-aged medical professional, was familiar with the concept of kink. I actually had a handout I'd made that I gave patients like this, going through safety concerns specific to pregnancy (for example, choking is never safe, but you *really* need to knock it off when you're pregnant since your air is your baby's air and your baby didn't consent). It had a bit at the bottom saying, *Sometimes intimate-partner violence starts during pregnancy, and consensually kinky relationships are not immune from abuse* and then went through the usual warning signs of an abusive relationship with some additions like *ignores your limits/boundaries*, and *disregards safewords.*

After the woman with the whip marks was gone, I told Sarah I needed to go to the bathroom and sat on the toilet, leaning my head against the wall. I felt guilty about not asking more questions, and told myself, *This woman isn't my patient, I didn't agree to any of this, I need to just cooperate as best I can and be ready for any opportunity I have to get out.*

If she can't leave either, then I can help her by escaping.

Even if she *could* leave, possibly I could help her, along with all the children here, by escaping. I was having a hot flash, and I turned on the sink to run cold water over my hands. I imagined a SWAT team coming to arrest Sarah, Brandon, Pastor John, and Ethan. Since this was a fantasy, I imagined Emma and Janet meekly surrendering, Joy ecstatically seeking proper care, Bethany weeping with delight over an armload of books.

"Are you almost done in there?" Sarah called. "We have another patient."

I washed my hands properly, dried them, and came out of the bathroom. Looked over the patient, who was one of the older women. "How can I help you today?" I asked.

On Fridays, I sat with Emma, Janet, Natalie, and Heather and stitched. I learned how to darn socks so they wouldn't give anyone a blister. I listened to Heather and Emma trade gossip until Natalie coughed disapprovingly. I learned the names of people's children and got Sarah's personal history. I'd noticed that when men and women went anywhere together, generally it was married couples, so I'd figured Brandon had to be her husband, but they really lacked that "married couple" vibe. Courtesy of bits and pieces from Emma, I learned that Sarah had originally joined the cult with a different spouse, a guy named Jeremy. He'd been part of the group that originally came to Harvest, along with their two children, but he'd left six months later, taking their children with him, and apparently he'd run away with Brandon's wife. Pastor John had announced that both Sarah's marriage to Jeremy and Brandon's marriage to his former wife were invalid now and had instructed Sarah and Brandon to marry each other and "be fruitful." So far, however, no fruit had resulted, and Emma was pretty sure that this was because Brandon was "stubborn," but Heather thought it was just that Sarah was old. Sarah was almost forty, which is in that gray area for fertility that I privately call the Murphy Zone, after Murphy's Law. If you *want* to get pregnant, you'll probably have trouble; if you *don't* want to get pregnant and take chances, you are 100 percent going to find yourself knocked up. So it really could be either.

Via mending-corner gossip, I'd also found out that Sister Caroline, who led the women's Bible study, was Pastor John's wife. Joy's mother had disappeared years earlier, from Benediction, their prior community, which was apparently less isolated than this one. Joy had been her mother's only child. Caroline had a brood of six or seven, although her last had been born well before the move to Harvest.

Joy usually worked in the kitchen, but as her pregnancy progressed she started swapping into the mending corner, which displaced Emma to the food prep task, to both Emma's irritation and Janet's. When Joy was replacing Emma, Natalie was a little more willing to leave us unsupervised, setting aside her work for long trips to the bathroom that I suspected were more about snatching time for herself than about a need for a higher-fiber diet, but who knows. On Fridays, I also did "deep bows before the Lord" and "lifted my face to the mountains" and "leaned into the Lord" and relaxed in "Lazarus pose." And then sat with everyone at women's Bible study, thinking about how hard it was to "study" a text you could not simply reread.

Saturday was the pediatric clinic, where I made recommendations for children that went mostly ignored.

Bethany's glasses came—Brandon did a post office trip along with the feed pickup, apparently—and she did her best to use them. I identified several children with fine or gross motor delays, another who needed glasses, and one who was much smaller than he should have been. This cult believed in vaccinating, thank goodness.

And then Sunday, church day. Worship and singing, "religious education" for me with the children, "Bible stories" from Joy that might or might not be Bible stories, the prayer circle where any child with an actual complaint was told not to complain, and girls were taught to use their "gentle voice," the saccharine tones all the women here used for literally everything.

Between prayer requests and mending-corner gossip, I pieced together some odds and ends of interpersonal information that seemed like they *could* be useful, maybe, somehow. Emma seemed to have the best relationship with her husband, of the women I saw regularly. She seemed to genuinely like and trust Jason. This didn't seem to be true of Janet, who seemed deeply sad, and not just about her infertility. On one occasion, in a brittle voice, she asked for people to pray for her to have help to show a sunny disposition, and a joyful countenance when she looked at her husband. This seemed like something I could potentially build on if I ever had the chance to speak with her alone, but I didn't.

The other thing I learned, which was satisfying if not exactly useful, was that no one liked the food.

I saw absolutely no phones. I saw absolutely no computers other than the one that Sarah would unlock for ultrasounds, which I used only under close supervision and which, I discovered when I did a little plausibly deniable poking around, had no Internet connection anyway. I thought there had to be phones, Internet, *some* connection to the outside world *somewhere*. Pastor John's office, maybe. They were selling things on Etsy! Someone had to be maintaining the Etsy site! But that office was kept locked when he wasn't in it. The keys were carried by him and a couple of the men. I might *eventually* reach the point where people forgot to be careful around me and I was able to get my hands on a key, sneak out in the night, and get into his office. But it seemed entirely possible that *even if that happened* I'd get in there and discover that the sole data connection was turned off and passworded.

The vehicles were also kept locked up in one of the outbuildings I'd seen my first day. There was the pickup truck used for feed delivery; there was the minivan that had been used to kidnap me, which was also used for grocery shopping. I heard from Emma that there was a small red Lexus that was Pastor John's personal car, but it hadn't been out in a while, and there was also a fifteen-passenger van that didn't run, sitting in the barn waiting for some part.

The vehicles I saw out most often were the four-wheelers used by men and older boys for various agricultural tasks, especially herding the cattle, and the golf cart they'd used as a snowplow, which they also used to haul stuff around on the compound (it had a flat bed in the back and looked like a miniature pickup truck). They called the golf cart the Gator, and when it was clean and the vivid green color of it was visible, it looked kind of like a toy car. I thought that if I had an opportunity to grab a vehicle and make a run for it, one of those vehicles was the most likely. The four-wheelers were loud and would be quickly noticed; the Gator didn't seem to go very fast. All of them were locked up at night, and if I took one of the four-wheelers, the odds that someone would quickly catch up to me on the other one seemed not in my favor, especially since I'd never used one before. I tried to at least observe enough that I'd be able to drive it if I had a chance.

Every now and then, I saw something up in the sky: mostly planes, occasionally agricultural drones, and I mulled over the possibility of climbing up onto the roof of the community building in the night to spray-paint *KIDNAPPED, SEND HELP* where the planes could see it and the community members couldn't. I had taken to stepping outside every time I had a hot flash in the night, so that maybe they'd get used to that and stop watching me so closely, and it was maybe *slightly* working. The night guard these days only came over if I left my porch. But that still left several missing steps, like finding a ladder to get on the roof, and finding spray paint to mark the roof.

Outsiders *never* came to the ranch, as far as I could tell. It was possible someone came in once every six months or once a year and I just hadn't seen them come yet, although if there was some necessary service that happened periodically, like propane delivery or septic-tank pumping, they'd probably have the foresight to keep me under guard while it was happening.

Just in case, though, I managed to filch a sheet of printer paper, tore it into neat quarters, and used my pen to write a note, which I kept in my bra so it would be ready to hand if the opportunity presented itself to give it to someone:

> *HELP. My name is Elizabeth Gwinn. I am a doctor and I was kidnapped by this group from my home in St. Paul, MN. Please call my father at 701-555-8246 and tell him where I am.*

One "Marketplace Day," I got whisked away from sanding to attend to someone who'd injured himself with a woodworking tool. My first thought was that if he'd severed a limb, they would *surely* have to take him somewhere else to get care, and if I'd thought about it in advance I could have written a note to slip into his clothes where some other doctor would find it. It turned out to be an ugly gash from a chisel slipping, and not an injury from a bandsaw; I cleaned it out, stitched it, and gave the injured man a tetanus shot. And then I wrote myself a second note, just in case:

> *HELP. This person is part of a group that kidnapped me. My name is Elizabeth Gwinn and I'm a doctor who was taken from my home in MN. Please call my father, Lt. Colonel (Air Force, retired) Sam Gwinn, 701-555-8246. Tell him I'm alive.*

In that note, I tried really hard to make sure I wouldn't put this hypothetical other doctor in a quandary about patient privacy that would discourage action. If I could get them to call my father, this would put other pieces into motion—law enforcement, warrants, whatever—that would obviate any dilemmas around HIPAA.

Ink can fade quickly, especially if you're carrying it next to your skin, but I took some of the pre-cut patches from the mending basket, and sandwiched the notes inside a thin layer of cotton broadcloth to protect them.

I had a final idea for a note. On a piece of paper I wrote simply *701-555-8246 SAM.*

If I had the opportunity to beg someone here for a favor, anyone who left, anyone who might have access to a phone, ever—I could give them my father's phone number. Maybe that would be enough. Maybe.

During the day, the cult kept me busy. At night, in bed, was when I had time—not to think, exactly. I had time to think during the day, to observe and consider whether I might be able to grab one of the four-wheelers without being seen right away, whether I could plant a "help me" note somewhere that it would fall out while Emma was grocery shopping without her noticing, a thousand possibilities that passed through my head and ended in *that won't work*. At night, I had time to stew. I had time to marinate in my anxiety, to face all the what-ifs I could just avoid thinking about most of the time when there was work to be done and I could keep moving. *What if I never get out of here?* What if no one's looking for me? What if years pass, and I never have an opportunity, or what if they break my spirit so badly I can't even try?

Thinking about my father sometimes turned into imagining someone at his funeral, some family friend delivering the eulogy because I wasn't there, talking about how he never recovered from the disappearance of his daughter. My parents had a series of miscarriages before they had me, and although they'd both wanted a bunch of kids, wound up settling for one.

Some nights I would find myself thinking about the day I was kidnapped, beating myself up for drinking that soda, for going to the interview. For not coming up with a better plan in the car, like getting my hands on a phone to call 911. Sometimes I'd feel a surge of fury at the people at the gas station who laughed when I tried to climb out, who just took the word of my kidnappers that I was a drug addict on my way to rehab, because they were white and respectable and middle-class looking.

Any of these spirals was just . . . not good. It wasn't good for planning, it wasn't good for sleeping, there wasn't any point to it, and I knew it and that didn't help. I started trying to deliberately redirect my thoughts when they'd get caught in one of these tracks, telling myself, *I have to stay ready, but I will get out of here.* Sometimes I would bring a page from *The Onyx Dagger* into my mind's eye, the one where I'd underlined a single sentence in crooked blue ballpoint: *there must be a way.*

CHAPTER 6

My third Monday in Harvest, I got through all the pregnant women in the morning, letting me linger in the community after lunch when Emma and Jason arrived with the groceries. I pushed aside my mug of coffee and went to help unload. My current goal was to try to spot where the keys got stored, and acting generally helpful in situations where everyone was pitching in was in line with my general goal of soothing everyone into relaxing their guard around me.

I was not directly monitored *all* the time: they clearly trusted the weather, and the isolation of the ranch, to keep me from getting far if I suddenly took off. I was never alone with my patients: Sarah was always there as well, with the sole exception of timid Chloe. Sock mending and wood sanding happened in groups; I'd wondered whether Emma could be persuaded to send a message to my father—*just let him know I'm alive, he's old, he deserves to know I'm not dead*—but I'd never had an opportunity to talk with her without several other people present.

The only person I'd really been able to chat with *alone* was Bethany. Bethany had started contriving to come hang out next to me during outdoor breaks on Sundays, to ask me for stories. I'd narrated the plot of *The Onyx Dagger*, and had moved on to the plot of *Star Wars*. I was debating whether to ask Bethany if she'd ever seen a phone here, and if so who had it, but I was constantly aware that Bethany might have an attack of conscience and confess who-knows-what, and get both of us into trouble.

She was such a sweet kid. Clingy, but sweet. Well, except to her brother. That day's lunch had been PB&J sandwiches, only we were running short of jam. Bethany had been in line ahead of JJ and had snatched the jar with the last of the grape jelly before JJ could get to it. JJ had cried, and Emma had resolved this by taking the jelly from both of them and handing it to the mom in line behind them, to give to her kids. Plain peanut butter sandwiches aren't very good. I both sympathized with Bethany about this and kind of agreed with Emma that she probably could have shared out that last little bit with JJ.

Bethany was staring at the table as I drank my coffee; I could see her feelings of guilt and shame like a little storm cloud over her head. Worried where that spiral might lead, I tried to think of a way to divert her. "Do you think there might be dessert tonight?" I asked.

She looked up and tried to school her own expression into something more cheerful. "Well, it's Brother Ethan's birthday," she said. "So probably yes."

I knew it was Ethan's birthday; there'd been a special morning prayer for him. "I've noticed that some birthdays get cake and some don't," I said.

"Elders always get cake," Bethany said. "Brother Ethan isn't an elder right now because he doesn't have a wife right now. But he *had* a wife, and she died. It wasn't that he wasn't a faithful husband. He was as faithful as he could be, don't you think?"

I made a noncommittal noise.

"What do you think of Brother Ethan?"

What I thought of Brother Ethan was definitely not something I could share uncensored with Bethany, even if we weren't within earshot of several other women. "I, hmm. I don't really know any of the men here very well. He's never come to me for medical care."

"He was a very faithful husband," Bethany said, again. Then she sat up straight and said, "Oh, I think my mom and dad are back with the groceries!"

I wanted to see where the keys went—this was going to be harder with Bethany glued to my side. Fortunately, as we went out to help bring them in, Bethany got called away to mind someone's toddler. I did a quick check; no one was *particularly* looking at me, though a half dozen other women were right nearby.

Plastic Walmart bags were tucked into big blue plastic crates; frozen goods were packed inside a big blue cooler.

I started lifting bags out and stringing the handles over my wrists and spotted, in the bottom of the crate, a little slip of paper that looked like a receipt.

My hand darted in and I had it in my fist, and then I grabbed two more bags (Walmart packs light bags) and started walking back up to the kitchen where they stored all the food. I didn't think anyone had seen me grab it, and I tried not to get my hopes up. What I was *hoping* I'd grabbed was a receipt that would give me a clue as to where I was. But it might have been an unused coupon, a grocery list, even just one of those receipts that had nothing useful on it. Putting the groceries down in the kitchen, I slipped it into my pocket as I pivoted.

Another trip and all the groceries were unloaded, so I sat down to pick up my abandoned, now-tepid coffee, and contrived to accidentally spill it down my shirt, giving me an ironclad excuse to return to my own room. With some apologies for making Sister Kate's life harder—Kate was in charge of the laundry—I went back to my room and shed my dress, grabbing the paper out of my pocket as I tugged it off.

I believed they had a camera in my room and probably also in my bathroom, modesty be damned, but I did not think they had put a camera in the wardrobe where my clothes hung, so I tucked myself inside so my body would block the camera's view and unfolded the paper to see what it was.

It was a receipt for gas bought at Terreton One Stop, on E 1500 N, Terreton, Idaho.

My surge of excitement at *finally knowing where I was,* approximately—even if it didn't tell me how to get away—was so strong that I almost missed another detail about that receipt. The person had paid ten dollars over the cost of the gas with a debit card, and received cash back.

I recognized this tactic; I knew exactly which places in Minot would give you cash back on a debit card purchase, because when I was talking to a woman whose spouse controlled all the money, it was something I regularly suggested. Start buying your gas at one of the places that does this and just get ten dollars in cash back each time. Keep the cash somewhere he won't find it. Or do it at the grocery store, although spouses like this were more likely to check grocery receipts. Gas receipts are easy to lose.

Emma and Jason shopped together. But their children, Bethany and JJ, did not come on grocery runs; they stayed back at the compound.

Was Emma trying to leave? Were they *both* trying to leave? In my excitement over spotting a receipt, I'd missed seeing where the keys went, although I'd seen Jason walking toward Pastor John's office. Could Emma be an ally? *How many people here* were not really here voluntarily?

THAT WEDNESDAY, I WAS pulled away from wood sanding again because a woman was in labor: Donna, having her sixth child. She'd expected it to go very quickly, but the baby's position was suboptimal and she was having back labor. Then we got word that another woman, Holly, was bleeding. Holly wasn't anywhere near delivery yet—she was probably having a miscarriage.

"Why don't you stay here with Sister Donna," I said to Sarah. "I'll go take a look at Sister Holly. Maybe she can just stay home, and I'll keep an eye on things there."

Sarah hesitated, looked at Donna, and then nodded permission.

I packed up the fetal Doppler and four tablets of misoprostol and went to Holly's house. Her husband wasn't there, of course. She had four children, and I saw them being hustled away by one of the teenage girls as I arrived. Natalie, the older woman from the mending circle who I had come to think of as Natalie, Killer of Fun, was making up Holly's bed with waterproof sheets and spreading out a blanket on her sofa that was fleece on one side, waterproof material on the other. My father used one of those on his couch back when he had an aging dog that had started losing bladder control in his sleep.

Natalie had brought along a basket of sewing and she sat down while I asked Holly when the bleeding had started. I wasn't sure if she was here as company for Holly or supervision for me. Probably both. I took out the Doppler to listen for a fetal heartbeat.

There was none; Holly was, in fact, miscarrying. She accepted the dose of misoprostol and settled down to wait. "You can go back to your other patient if you want," she said.

"I'd like to keep an eye on you for a little while," I said. "Sarah will send someone if she needs my help with Donna."

"I'm probably just going to lie down and take a rest," she said.

"That's fine," I said.

Natalie hummed a hymn, and we sat together for a

while. I thought about stories I could tell Bethany when I finished with *Star Wars*. Should I go to *Empire Strikes Back* or try something else? What else did I remember well enough to narrate? Maybe *The Princess Bride*. Unless she'd already seen it, back before her family joined a cult.

As soon as it seemed reasonable, I excused myself to the bathroom. Anytime I was somewhere outside my own little hut, I tried to make a quick search of the bathroom in the hopes of finding a hidden cell phone. Just about the only thing people did alone here was visit the toilet, and they'd said Turkey "found a way" to look at porn—maybe there were phones hidden.

There was a medicine cabinet over the sink: no phone there. There was a bottle of zolpidem, a sleeping pill that could be habit-forming, and some everyday stuff like chewable antacids. The zolpidem had clearly been dispensed by Sarah; it was in a bottle that had previously held ibuprofen, with a hand-lettered label of instructions taped over top.

I turned on the water to disguise the noise and lifted off the top of the toilet tank. Toilet tanks were a classic hiding place for illegal drugs, and to my genuine shock, there was something in there, sealed inside a ziplock bag, and I started shaking with excitement as I tried not to drop the tank lid. But it wasn't a phone. It was a book. I pulled out the bag, opened it, and took a look.

It was a romance novel called *The Duke of the Duck Pond*, sort of Regency-ish. I could tell from the cover and the spine that this book had been read over and over and over. I flipped through quickly but there were no notes or anything else inside. I had found Holly's secret, but it wasn't a secret I could use to get away; it was Holly's *Onyx*

Dagger. I was briefly tempted to take it to read myself, but my room was searched regularly. They'd probably find it and confiscate it before I could finish reading it, anyway.

I sealed it up in its ziplock bag and tucked it back in the tank, set the lid in place, and turned off the water. Natalie and Holly were both where I'd left them: Natalie on the couch, Holly in her bed.

The bright afternoon slowly wore on. I stared out the window at the distant mountains, thinking about romance novels. Back in Minot, I used to swap them with Sue, one of the labor nurses. She was more into the contemporary kind with good banter than the kind with bodices that could get ripped, although she'd happily read Regencies with good banter, as well. We'd switched to e-readers at around the same time, which unfortunately made it harder to share books. Sue had retired a couple of years ago, but came to my trial. "To glare at the witnesses against you," she said, in the email she sent to let me know she'd be there. "You won't see me because you'll have your back to the people watching, so just know I'm there, glaring."

As the sun dipped low, Bethany brought a basket to the house with dinner for all three of us, but she didn't stay. Holly didn't feel much like eating and after she reiterated three times that she didn't want her slice of shepherd's pie, Natalie ate it, saying she didn't want it to go to waste. I drew the curtains and lowered the lights.

If I had a cell phone and wanted to hide it in this room, where would I hide it? Under the mattress was a terrible place to hide anything, if you expected someone to search. Under the bed was even worse, although maybe if you had children's clothes stored in a box, as they probably did, someone could hide a phone under the clothes. There was a dresser against the wall: secured to the back of a drawer would actually be a *good* hiding place. Or secured to the underside of the couch . . .

I heard someone snoring. Natalie had stretched out on the couch, put her head on a pillow, and gone to sleep. Holly—well, she *looked* asleep, though it was hard to tell for sure. If there was a phone, a laptop, anything like that, somewhere *other* than the bathroom, now was my chance to search. And I could open the drawers to that dresser, and if I woke anyone up, I could claim I was looking for a blanket to drape over Natalie.

I crossed the room as silently as I could and eased the drawer open. Glanced over at the two women again. Reached to the back of the drawer—

And found a phone, secured with a strip of duct tape to the back of that drawer, just like I'd imagined.

Stifling my own gasp, I stuffed it in my pocket and gently closed the drawer, then shut myself into the bathroom. There was a towel hanging up, still a little damp, and I wrapped it around the phone as I pressed the on button, because sometimes cell phones chime when you turn them on. This one made no noise; it just vibrated in my hand as it started up.

I'd spent a lot of time thinking about what I'd do with a cell phone—specifically, I'd thought about whether my first move should be calling 911. Calls to 911 were routed to the local authorities; how well did those authorities get along with this cult? Would they arrive in force, or would they send a single person to check in and go away if the cult told them to? Would the cult cooperate or would they fight back? I was old enough to remember the Branch Davidians in Waco. It was easy to imagine a thousand ways that a 911 call could go horribly wrong.

But also: I was worried about being overheard, and when the phone came to life, it showed almost no service. Texts would probably work; a phone call might or might not.

If it had been locked, I would have had no choice but to call 911. But it wasn't locked.

I sent my father a text. Dad? It's Lizzie.

No response. My dad went to bed early these days because he woke up at five. With the time difference, he'd probably gone to sleep hours ago.

Don't reply to this, I'm using a stolen cell phone. I was kidnapped. Someone lured me with a job interview and then drugged me. I think I'm in Idaho, near Terreton. On a cult compound. The minivan's license plate is MJM-446, and I can walk around the compound but they won't let me leave. This is the first time I've had access to a cell phone. They kidnapped me so they'd have an OBGYN. They kidnapped another doctor and then murdered her because she wouldn't help.

I thought about what else I could tell him.

The compound is at the end of a long driveway and there's a green gate. A big community building and a bunch of small houses. We're far enough back from the road I can't see traffic. I found a receipt from the Terreton One Stop, that's why I think we're near there.

Don't reply to this.

Could I just keep this phone? Would they notice? I checked the sent texts: Holly appeared to turn it on once a week to send a quick text to her own parents, telling them everything was fine and giving an update on the kids. If she stuck to that schedule it would be a few days, but given that she was having a miscarriage I didn't want to count on that.

I heard a rustle outside the bathroom, which sent a spike of fear through my body.

My hands were shaking, making it hard to text. I deleted my sent texts, marked Dad's number as spam in case my dad replied anyway, and then turned the phone off and stuffed it in my sleeve.

Everyone was still asleep when I came out of the bathroom, and I got the phone back where I'd found it just in time; footsteps came up the porch. Natalie jolted back up into a sitting position as Sarah knocked quietly on the door. "Donna's home with her baby," she said. "You can go home and sleep, I'll take over here."

I nodded. A quiet young man escorted me back to my own house, and I lay in bed, wide-eyed from adrenaline, until it was late enough that I could imagine my father, hundreds of miles away, reading my texts. *At least he'll know I'm in trouble.*

At least he'll know I'm alive.

Joy was in the next day for a checkup. She was now far enough along that if she had a preterm delivery somewhere with a NICU, the baby would probably be okay, but of course, we had no NICU. She'd been having contractions, irregular but painful. I checked her cervix, which remained high and tight, just like you'd want to see at that point in someone's third trimester. "These are Braxton Hicks contractions," I told her. "Normal, even though they're annoying."

"They're your uterus getting ready to do its job," Sarah said brightly. I refrained from pointing out that it was a job we weren't going to be able to let it do, given the baby's position.

"I can't sleep," Joy said. "If I'm not waking up to pee, I'm waking up because of one of these contractions."

"We could give you something like Benadryl, or Unisom . . ." I started to say, thinking of the zolpidem I'd seen in the medicine cabinet last night, but Sarah was shaking her head.

"Brother David doesn't approve of medications in pregnancy unless they're absolutely necessary," she said.

"Hmm," I said. That's what I'd started saying whenever they told me something unhinged. "Sister Joy, are you still doing the usual amount of work?" She nodded. "I'm going to prescribe some extra rest for you. You can nap, or you can sit down with your feet up, whatever's most comfortable. If you get a little extra sleep, so much the better, but we don't want these contractions *turning* into preterm labor, and extra rest will help."

It doesn't, actually, but Joy needed extra rest for her own sake, and I'd trotted out the "it's better for the baby" white lie a thousand times in my normal life, I could certainly do it here.

It was snowing, and all the teenagers, including Bethany, were outside with shovels when I went up to lunch. When we came out, most of their work had been undone by the ongoing snowfall. I stood outside the community building for a long minute when I came out after lunch, listening. I could hear one of the children shrieking (he'd just gotten a face full of snowball) and doors slamming and farther away, the rumbling buzz of one of the ATVs. I could hear birds.

If my father woke up this morning and saw the texts, and immediately called the police, it was still too early for them to be coming. This involved multiple states, so that would require the FBI, I was pretty sure, and they'd probably need time to figure out exactly where I was. The absolute soonest was probably tomorrow. It might be longer.

I looked up at the falling snow and told myself, *Sleep when they let you sleep, eat when they let you eat, prepare any way you can, be ready.*

Thursday afternoon was quiet. Word had made it back to me that the asthmatic boy was being given a task outside the chicken barn, so at least I probably wouldn't be called on to handle a teenager in respiratory failure this week. Since not a lot of people were coming by, I started going through the drug stocks to check expiration dates, since I did not trust that Sarah was checking on this. In late afternoon we got a very timid knock at the door that turned out to be Bethany. She took a deep breath and said, "I'm not here for medical treatment, everything's fine, I was just thinking." She paused. I glanced at Sarah, a little worried that Bethany was going to bring up our fiction-based relationship, especially since Bethany was getting increasingly pink. "I would like to train as a midwife," she said. "With Sister Sarah and Dr. Elizabeth. Would that be okay?"

Bethany, you are thirteen, I thought. That might not

matter here; she might be considered fully old enough for professional training. I was fond of Bethany; if she was close to me, I could try to keep her safe when the rescue came—if it came. But this still struck me as a terrible idea.

Sarah was speaking. "Have you discussed this with your father, Bethany? Or Pastor?"

"I haven't," Bethany said. "Because I wanted to start by asking if it would be all right with both of *you*."

"You never seemed interested before," Sarah said, and her eyes flicked toward me, briefly.

"I brought dinner last night to Sister Holly, Sister Natalie, and Dr. Elizabeth, and when I left, I thought, 'I should be staying,' and I realized it was God, speaking in my heart."

I was so relieved she had not stayed. A bright-eyed apprentice would have made it much harder to search for a phone. "Remind me how old you are?" I asked.

"I'll be turning fourteen in March."

"Bethany, let me tell you a little bit about the training I had. I'm a doctor, not a midwife. When I was your age, I was in middle school. After that, I went to high school. Then, I went to college, where I majored in chemistry, and after *that* I went to medical school for four years, after which I did a residency, which was my actual apprenticeship in obstetrics and gynecology. I'm not saying that you cannot learn useful skills at your age, but is there really nothing else your school can teach you?"

There was a long pause and I thought, *Not without books, of course, that's why her school is useless to her.*

"Talk to your father and have him talk to Pastor John and Brother Ethan," Sarah said. "With their permission, you may start sitting in with us as the opportunity presents itself. Probably you will mostly be sent on errands, for now."

Bethany's face split into a huge smile. "Thank you! I'll let you get back to work!" And she darted off.

"Really?" I said, when she was gone. "You aren't worrying about traumatizing that nice child with the blood, the screaming, all the rest?"

Another half glance. "My mother had her last four children at home, and I was there for all four. I didn't wind up traumatized."

I wondered how to even answer that. *Maybe if you hadn't been traumatized as a teenager you wouldn't have grown up to join a cult and kidnap people. Though who knows.* I went with, "Experiences vary."

"She'll be able to leave if she wants to."

"I wanted to be a doctor starting when I was about the age Bethany is now. No one invited me to sit in on surgery, and that was *good.* I had time to mature before I was faced with the realities of my profession. If someone had invited me to sit in on a birth when I was thirteen . . ." I paused and tried to imagine it. ". . . I might have become a doctor still, but I'd have gone for a different specialty."

"If it's her calling, she'll be fine."

"Are you *hoping* to scare her off?"

"Of course not," Sarah said.

"Are you worried that a well-trained apprentice will make you *replaceable*?"

"I brought *you* here," Sarah said. "You're more trained than I am."

"I mean, yes," I said, "but I didn't make you replaceable, because for one thing, they want you keeping an eye on me." Sarah looked down. "Bethany won't be fully trained for years, but once she is, she could take over for you."

"That's why it's a good idea to train her, and the sooner the better. What if something happens to me?" She paused. "To both of us?"

I dropped the subject and decided I'd need to come up with a list of errands to send Bethany on, if I needed to get her out of the room. I returned to the expiration-date audit. Most of the drugs were within something resembling a reasonable tolerance, but there were also a dozen packs of antibiotics that expired two years ago. I set them aside. "These should be replaced," I said.

"I'll let Pastor know," Sarah said.

Something from the earlier conversation was nagging at me. "Why does Brother Ethan get a say in Bethany's apprenticeship?" I asked.

"Because he's her betrothed," Sarah said.

"He's—what?"

"He's going to be her husband," Sarah said. "Because he's widowed, since Ginny died, and Bethany will be old enough soon."

Bethany's chatter about Ethan, and how he'd been a *faithful husband*, and wanting to know what I thought of him, rushed back to me, and I felt fully lightheaded. "How soon?"

"When she turns fourteen. So, March. Don't worry, Dr. Elizabeth. Brother Ethan was a very good husband to Ginny."

Brother Ethan is a murderer, I thought. And Bethany was a *child*. Literally a child. "Bethany is not physically mature," I said, knowing that I was betraying my thoughts with my voice.

"She started menstruating when she was twelve," Sarah said. "I've tracked her growth, and she's as grown as she's going to get. Anyway, we trust that if a girl's body is not ready to bear children, she won't get pregnant."

"You literally had me examine a girl because she wasn't pregnant yet."

"Everyone knew something odd was going on with Sister Chloe and Brother Nick. And we were right. Brother Nick wasn't doing a proper job of it."

Our conversation was interrupted by a knock: two people had sore shoulders from shoveling snow. I forced a smile to my face as I gave them ibuprofen and ice packs.

How long will it take? I thought. *Surely my father will go to the police. Surely the police will go to the FBI. Surely the FBI will find us—I narrowed it down for them! And there's probably some way they can trace the phone the message came from? When it turns on the next time, they can get a fix on the location. Surely it will only be a few more days.*

Taking the phone with me would have been a foolish risk, but it would have let me text *with* my father, and I was gripped with a sudden, intense longing to hear his voice. I remembered our last conversation, right before I was kidnapped: *You never think people like you. You'll be even farther from home. Love you.*

What if something had happened to him? He was an old man, what if the shock of my disappearance had—

No. I refused to let myself spiral into that possibility. Someone would be coming. I just had to wait. I just had to be patient.

Lying in bed that night, I thought about Isabelle, and how the story in *The Onyx Dagger* is all from Deirdre's perspective, not Isabelle's. The reader never finds out how Isabelle felt after her capture, before she was hypnotized; how long she fought the mind powers of Lord Nightshade; whether she trusted that rescue was coming. Whether she listened to the screams and cries of other prisoners and wasn't able to save them any more than she could save herself. Whether she tried not to give up.

It was a shame that none of that was in the book, I thought, because that felt like what I needed, just now.

I SPENT ALL OF Friday listening for what I imagined rescue would sound like: cars, lots of them, driving closer. Or a helicopter. Probably not a helicopter, but if I *heard* a helicopter, probably a helicopter. I listened as I stitched. I listened as I "bowed down before the Lord." I listened as I told Bethany the plot of *Star Trek II: The Wrath of Khan*.

I heard an agricultural drone pass overhead once. Every single vehicle motor I heard turned out to be the cult's ATVs.

Dinner was black bean and ham soup with bread, and something was going on. There was markedly less conversation than I usually heard at dinner, and everyone was avoiding everyone else's eyes. It was Friday, so time for "Testimonies and Confessions," and I wondered if someone was confessing something particularly big. Bethany seemed subdued but not nervous, so hopefully that meant she wasn't planning to confess our shared stories.

Dinner finished, and Holly and her husband stood up.

Oh shit, I thought. *This is about the cell phone.*

The cell phone, and also the romance novel. Holly confessed, weeping, to both, as I wondered if I hadn't been careful enough, if *I* was the reason they'd been discovered? Had Natalie overheard the toilet lid, had she reported it, had this set off a search? Holly handed over the cell phone and the book: the cell phone was solemnly placed onto a concrete block and then smashed with a hammer. The book was ripped into sections, doused with something, and set on fire.

Will anyone remember that I was unsupervised while at Holly's house? I wondered. It was just a few days ago. I saw Natalie glance over at me. She knew she'd fallen asleep. She could *confess* to having fallen asleep. She was probably *supposed* to confess to having fallen asleep.

But Pastor John was angry. Frighteningly angry. Bethany was sitting to my left, her face very pale, and Janet was to my right, her arms wrapped around herself. Holly was kneeling on the floor, sobbing, and Pastor John laid his hand on her head and said, "I cast *out* the demon of disobedience. I cast it *out*. Sister Holly, you cannot open the door just a tiny crack to Satan's influence. When you open that door, you let Satan into your life. And what did Satan take in return? *He took your child.*"

He was talking about the miscarriage. *You piece of shit*, I thought.

"It's time to drive out the demon. I'm placing you in the hands of the Elders."

"No," she sobbed, as three of the men picked her up off the floor and dragged her into the room where we changed for our fitness classes. The door slammed shut behind them.

"Joy," Pastor John said, and she rose to lead a hymn.

We heard the swish-crack of a blow with something like a cane, and a scream.

"Amazing grace, how sweet the sound," Joy sang, and around me, everyone shakily joined in.

"In the name of Christ Jesus I cast out the demon of fear," I heard a man's voice intone, through the door. Another swish-crack. "In the name of Christ Jesus I cast out the demon of disobedience." Holly was screaming, but it wasn't words, anymore, just screams of pain.

Next to me, I could see tears trickling down Bethany's cheeks.

Natalie was looking at me again, and this time, I thought, she was weighing whether or not *I* was going to confess anything that would get *her* into trouble. I tried to beam *I'm not going to narc on you, Natalie* straight into her brain.

"Oh God, have mercy—" I heard Holly's voice cut off in another guttural scream as whoever was wielding the cane hit her four or five times in a row.

She is my patient. She miscarried less than a week ago. I have to do something.

I didn't think it would do any good for me to intervene. I told myself that if I thought it would help, I would *have* to, but it wouldn't. I thought about how later, if I had the chance to talk to Holly, I would tell her that I once delivered a healthy full-term baby for a woman with a Baphomet tattoo on her left thigh, which ought to prove that miscarriages are not the result of a lack of faith in God. All me intervening was going to do was draw Pastor John's attention to me.

I was pretty sure, anyway.

So I stood, unprotesting, with everyone else, humming along with all seven verses of "Amazing Grace," until the song ended. Holly was allowed out of the room, and her husband was ordered into it, but we didn't have to stay and listen to his punishment.

Pastor John said, "I expect there are other secret phones here. Secret *books* here. I am declaring a period of grace and forgiveness for anyone who *voluntarily* turns over forbidden objects. You have until sundown tomorrow. You are dismissed."

Back in the relative safety of my house, I crawled under my blankets. I kept remembering the sound of the beating, the sound of Holly's screams, and nothing was pushing that memory out of my mind.

Dad, I need you to hurry, I thought.

Please hurry.

CHAPTER 7

I WANTED TO WEEP with frustration when I saw *two* cell phones turned in Saturday morning at breakfast, along with a dozen books. Instead of being showily destroyed, these books were all set aside in the locked storage room that turned out to be filled with books. The phones were turned on in order to do a factory reset and then locked up in Pastor John's office, and that made me think about the fact that the phone I'd used was smashed, possibly without being turned on again, making it impossible for anyone to get a fix on me. Also, I'd sent that message on Wednesday night, and now it was Saturday. On Monday, Jason and Emma were going to take the minivan to Walmart, so maybe—*maybe*—the fact that I'd included the license plate number would help the authorities track them back to me?

Or maybe this wasn't going to work.

Maybe I was going to have to sneak out on foot, come spring. But I wanted to get out *before* Bethany was given to Ethan as a "wife," and March weather was incredibly unpredictable. It could be spring or even summer weather one day, snowing the next. Weather forecasts were one more thing I didn't have access to here.

Between the gossip I heard from the women and the gossip I heard from the children, I was able to piece together what had happened: Holly's oldest son, a ten-year-old named Peter, had found the romance novel. He'd clogged the toilet and plunged it, but apparently took off the lid because he was worried it would overflow if he flushed it to see if the plunging had worked. He'd found the book, and had not confessed to Pastor John but had told his best friend, another ten-year-old boy, who had told his brother, a fourteen-year-old boy, who had told Pastor John.

Sitting in Sunday school, looking at the dark circles under Joy's eyes as she told everyone about Joseph's coat of many colors, I thought about how one of the ongoing themes in *The Onyx Dagger* was figuring out who you could trust. Deirdre herself had that +10 Charisma advantage of the protagonist in this sort of book; she could get people to trust her just by saying, "trust me," while looking deeply into their eyes. But that didn't mean she could necessarily trust them in return. She knew she could trust Isabelle, her lifelong friend (except when Isabelle was being mind-controlled) but as they gathered followers she realized she couldn't delegate *everything* to Isabelle, and she needed both to figure out who she could trust not to betray her, and who she could trust to be competent.

No one here trusts anyone else here, I thought.

That seemed a little hard to believe, so I examined it.

Not only was I routinely supervised, very few people here were allowed to spend time in pairs, except for married couples, and married couples were usually accompanied by their children. Except for Jason and Emma when they went out shopping, when their children were kept behind at the ranch.

Sarah and Brandon were trusted enough by Pastor John to leave, with the minivan, drive a thousand miles, and commit a kidnapping. That was quite a lot of trust. But it was about the only example of that I'd seen.

Well, and some of the men were allowed to carry guns. It wasn't all of them, though; it was the night watchmen and some of the agricultural workers. I saw the men so much less frequently than the women that I hadn't fully learned their names. I thought maybe a quarter of the adult men had guns at least some of the time. They didn't store them in their homes, though; the guns were yet another thing that got locked up back in the community building.

As we were watching the children run around during the break between morning and afternoon worship, an ag drone flew overhead, and I looked up at it, thinking, *Maybe I should revisit my idea about the roof.* Could I spell out *help* with clothing stolen from the laundry? Wet towels wouldn't blow away. Would that be visible? Would it be noticed too fast from the ground?

Joy was standing next to me; we were largely alone, the children distracted for the moment, and I said, "Joy, if you have any ideas for getting out of here, I'll help you any way I can."

Her head snapped to the side to look at me, and then she did a quick, paranoid survey of people in the area. No one was close enough to hear.

"I mean it," I said. "Tell me what to do and I'll do it."

She chewed on her lip and said nothing for a minute. Then someone else came over, and the chance to talk more was lost.

A WEEK AFTER I sent the texts to my father, I thought, *This didn't work.*

Something had gone wrong. I'd screwed up my dad's number (impossible to check now) or the texts hadn't gone through. Or the cops hadn't believed him or the information wasn't specific enough for the FBI to know where we were—maybe there were dozens of cults with compounds in this part of Idaho. *Probably* there were dozens of cults with compounds in this part of Idaho. Or maybe the receipt had been a red herring set out for me, specifically, and we weren't in Idaho at all.

I needed a new plan. I tried to think of one.

The people here were very careful with the car keys, and very careful with the phones and Internet connections. Even if I could get the key to the minivan, I'd also need the key to the barn where it was kept.

They were also careful with guns. Less careful than they were with cars, though. I *might* be able to get my hands on a gun, which might be loaded, and then I'd have however many shots were in the magazine.

On a dreary afternoon with very few patients, I envisioned myself with one of the hunting rifles. I stared out the window at the heavy skies that looked like they were full of snow that wasn't actually coming down yet. If I *did* get one of those rifles, I'd have to be willing to shoot people; they'd surely be able to tell, if I wasn't actually willing. *I am a doctor.* I thought I could shoot Pastor John, and I could shoot Brother Ethan. I could probably shoot Sarah.

I couldn't shoot someone who'd been one of my patients, and I thought about how many people here that was. They'd probably send some of the teenage boys to take me down. Clumsy but strong fifteen-year-olds. And count on my unwillingness to shoot anyone I saw as a child.

If it came right down to it, I wasn't even entirely sure I could shoot Pastor John.

Obstetricians don't generally treat bullet wounds, but during my month of emergency medicine during my internship rotations, there was a hunting accident and the victim got brought in. A man in his forties had been shot by a member of his own deer-hunting party because they lost track of one another and someone thought he was a deer. Alcohol was involved. The bullet hit him in the leg, and fortunately for him missed the femoral artery, but it shattered the bone. He survived the injury, but he lost the leg.

Medical careers are not a good path for the squeamish, but almost every nurse can tell you the *one thing* they just cannot handle. (I even know a few for whom it's vomit. They don't work in maternity.) For me, I looked at the horrifying mess that had been that man's left leg and thought, *Okay, wow, emergency care is not for me.* The human body does enough stupid bullshit all on its own, without bringing *high-velocity projectiles* into it.

If I don't think I can actually make myself shoot someone, there is no point in trying to steal a gun.

What did that leave?

If I found a phone again, I would call 911. If the call didn't go through, I would steal the phone and try again. That would require hiding it. I had no faith that I could come up with a hiding place in my room that wouldn't immediately be found, but my coat had an interior pocket that was hard to find, and my coat, for now, usually traveled with me.

I still had my *help me* notes, but I'd had no opportunities to pass them along. Unfortunately, my theory that they simply never had outsiders come to the compound seemed to be largely accurate.

I thought back to the day that one klutz had gouged himself with a chisel. I'd thought, briefly, that this might be a real emergency, something they couldn't just have me handle. Could I *fake* an emergency?

I could potentially *create* an emergency. I could probably start a kitchen fire, "accidentally," but they had hoses and fire extinguishers and would try to put out the fire themselves. Also, men didn't work in the kitchen; the person I was most likely to injure with a kitchen fire was Bethany. I was pretty sure that the only way I'd convince anyone here that an emergency hospital trip was *actually required* would be if one of the high-status men had the emergency.

I could sabotage the woodworking equipment. I thought about those woodworking lessons with my father that had petered out before we got to power tools, and how I didn't know enough about the equipment to know how to sabotage a safety feature, and how even if I could work out what to do, I could wind up maiming one of the teenage boys, who were woodworking novices and more likely to have an accident.

Back to that first idea. Could I convince some man that he was having a stroke or a heart attack? Could I convince Sarah, and Pastor John?

I mean, *ideally* I'd make Pastor John think *he* was having a heart attack. He had never visited the clinic; if he did, I could try convincing him that he had cancer. Melanoma, probably, since that's something I could plausibly spot even if he was actually in for something else.

But it probably wouldn't be Pastor John. The odds that I'd have someone else turn up with a panic attack were also not great, because surely my best chance at seeing a panic attack would have been in the days right after Holly's beating. (Panic attacks frequently cause chest pain and shortness of breath; it wouldn't be hard to convince someone having a panic attack that they were having a heart attack.) If someone turned up with a migraine, I *might* be able to convince them it was a stroke, but if they'd had migraines before that felt similar, they probably wouldn't believe me.

I tried to think through the other ways this could go wrong. If someone did have a medical emergency, the cult might still not take them anywhere—they might take them into the community house and pray over them. And if I'd lied about it being an emergency, the prayer would even "work." If they did decide they had to seek care, probably because the person with the emergency was sufficiently high status, they'd probably put them in the van and drive them to the hospital, not call an ambulance, and there's no way they'd bring me along, although they might bring Sarah. If I put my note on the person heading to the hospital, I had no way of ensuring it was found. And no way of ensuring it wasn't found by one of the cult members, who would certainly know I'd written the note.

What would they do to me, at that point? *No one wants you to get a thrashing, Doctor.* The noise of Holly's beating still echoed in my ears, sometimes.

Was it worth the risk?

I thought it might be worth the risk. But I'd need someone—one of the adult men, specifically—to turn up with a plausible emergency to put that plan into action.

JASON CAME TO THE clinic to discuss Bethany's desire for "apprenticeship." I could tell from looking at him that his knee was getting worse, not better, and when he settled into the folding chair Sarah brought out, his brow was furrowed.

"Bethany says she wants to apprentice with you," he said, speaking more to me than to Sarah. "Pastor said I should talk to you about it." He paused, then went on before I could reply. "I like the idea. She's a bright kid."

"And as the community grows, it will be good to have more women who can attend births," Sarah added. "We are to become a refuge for the faithful, after all."

"Right," Jason said. He looked a little listless. "Anyway, it's fine with me, so long as she stays out of the way, and doesn't ask questions that bother your patients."

"Can you let her know that if I ask her to leave, she needs to do it without delay?" I asked.

"Oh, you shouldn't have any problems with that," Jason said. "She's a good, obedient girl."

"What does Brother Ethan think?" Sarah asked.

There was a flicker of pain or anger in Jason's face, smoothed away to blankness so quickly I wasn't entirely sure if I'd imagined it. "Once they're married, it'll be his decision about whether she can continue. But I think he knows how important it is for there to be women trained to help with births."

"So you haven't talked with him about it?"

"Pastor might have, I don't know."

"All right," Sarah said, with a slightly perplexed smile. "It won't do any harm to let her start learning, even if Brother Ethan decides she should have other priorities."

"That's right," Jason said. He stood up, wincing a little as he straightened his leg. "I'll let her know she can start coming this afternoon."

Her father's approval gained, Bethany started turning up, bright-eyed and enthusiastic, every Monday, Thursday, and Saturday, as well as coming for part of the evening if we were sitting with a woman in labor.

There had been several births since I'd arrived. All the babies had come out without major problems so far, so my ability to do a field-hospital-style cesarean section was still untested. There'd been one woman who tore badly enough that she'd probably have had an easier time healing from a C-section; I'd stitched her up as carefully as I could, and told Sarah that this woman absolutely needed to rest as much as possible, her husband was not allowed to have sex with her until I explicitly lifted the restriction, and that I didn't care if she stood up on Sunday and blasphemed the Holy Spirit, absolutely no corporal punishment until she was entirely healed.

My fears about Bethany being freaked out by childbirth were so far unwarranted. Her first week, a woman named Vanessa did have a significant birth complication, shoulder dystocia. Usually, once the woman births the baby's head, the rest of the body slides out without any additional difficulty; the head is usually the biggest part, and in general, if a baby is just going to refuse to come out, it's the whole baby that gets stuck. In shoulder dystocia, the head comes out but the shoulders get stuck. This is arguably the only complication of childbirth where you're better off at home, since once the baby's head is out, it's too late to do a C-section anyway. Home births don't involve epidurals, and if a woman hasn't had medications that keep her from moving freely, you can do the Gaskin maneuver, where you have her get on all fours. I had to use a couple other tricks to get this baby out, but we got her out by the end, and afterward, as Sarah bathed the baby and gave it back to Vanessa while I checked over the placenta, I thought she had the self-satisfied smile of a kidnapper who now felt entirely justified in her kidnapping.

Bethany was focused on me rather than Sarah, and her eyes shone with hero-worship. I had to admit, if I'd gotten to watch someone get a stuck baby out back when I was thirteen, it would have made an impression on me, too.

We sent Bethany to tell Vanessa's husband when she was ready to go home, and then Sarah, Bethany, and I went up to the community house for our late dinner. Sometimes we'd take a light meal in the clinic if someone was in the middle of a delivery, but Vanessa had been in transition labor when the dinner bell rang, and I didn't think she'd be up for smelling lasagna. Bethany had run up to tell the cooks to set plates aside for us to eat later. The community house was dark and quiet when we got there. Sarah flipped on the lights, and then we went into the kitchen to reheat our food and eat it.

I hadn't spent a lot of time in the kitchen, and I glanced around as Bethany bustled around with the microwave, making my habitual set of assessments. Did I see a phone? (No.) A laptop? (No.) Any likely hiding spots for phones? (Plenty, but I couldn't search with Sarah sitting right there. Or Bethany, for that matter.) *Would* anyone hide something here? (Maybe; it would be inconvenient, and you'd risk your phone being found, but on the other hand, if someone found it, they wouldn't know whose it was.) Was there an obvious way to cause an emergency? (The stoves were all electric; it would be possible to start a fire, but not nearly as easy as it would be with gas. Also, again, not with Sarah right here.)

"Can you tell me what you did today?" Bethany asked, setting my food down in front of me.

I explained shoulder dystocia and the various ways to resolve it. Bethany listened with wide-eyed interest as I wished I had one of those models of a pelvis and a baby that childbirth educators sometimes used. When we were done eating, Bethany washed the dishes we'd used and Sarah dried them and put them away, and we walked Bethany back to her parents' house, and the night guard walked me back to mine.

I lay in bed, thinking about how at home, in my real life, I'd have to do charting, now. *If only they'd placed a fucking ad instead of doing a kidnapping. Wanted: ob-gyn to live on-site in rural Idaho. Payment: room and board. No insurance companies, no Epic Systems of any kind, and NO CHARTING EVER.*

I mean, the "also, no books" would be a dealbreaker for a lot of people. Unless they wanted to raise the pay significantly.

No charting ever, though. I'd have considered it.

I HAD A VIVID dream that night. In it, I had taken advantage of a medical emergency—it wasn't clear if it was an actual emergency or if I'd just pretended it was—to try to smuggle a note to an outside doctor, and the note had been found by Sarah. In the dream she came screaming out of the van that I'd sent the note, and I was grabbed by Ethan and dragged into that side room where they'd thrashed Holly for having a phone, and as I was bracing myself for a beating, they brought in Bethany and beat her instead, while I watched.

"If we thrashed *you*, you might be impaired when we need you to perform a surgery," Sarah explained. "So Bethany gets your thrashing."

In the dream, my screams mixed with Bethany's, but I was fixed in place, the way you sometimes are in dreams, completely unable to move to stop them.

I jerked awake, the image of Bethany's wide betrayed eyes still vivid in my mind, and sat up, terrified that I'd fall right back into that dream if I closed my eyes again. I went to the bathroom, wondering if this was a thing they actually did. Was it a thing I'd heard them mention doing, and forgot? Was my subconscious trying to remind me of something I'd actually heard about?

Sometimes husbands were beaten in their wife's place, that's what it was. Sarah had mentioned that, after I'd said Gwen needed to be excused from all physical punishments for several months—*Brother Ken can do it in her place if anything comes up.* Beyond that, my brain was probably just spinning horrors out of shadows.

I put on my coat and stepped outside in my slippers. It was a dark, clear, cold night, no moon and no clouds. I stepped away from the motion-detector porch light so I could look up at the stars, although the cold from the ground was seeping through the thin soles under my feet. I could spot the Big Dipper, and followed the pointer stars to the North Star, thinking about how, even if I could reliably navigate by the stars, I had no idea whether the nearest town was north, south, east, or west of here.

There was a drone somewhere overhead, I could hear it. I took my flashlight out of my pocket and blinked an SOS up at the sky, wishing I had learned enough Morse code to send a real message. Not that there was a particularly big chance that whichever farmer was using that drone to check on his herd would be looking for Morse code messages by flashlight. I blinked out SOS again anyway. And again.

I heard footsteps and wondered if someone had noticed my flashlight. I stuck it in my pocket as Ethan came around the corner. "What are you doing?" he asked.

"I'm looking at the stars," I said.

"Oh," he said, and looked up. "Yeah, it's a good night for it. Don't get too cold, now."

"I won't."

He went back to his post. I couldn't hear the drone anymore, and my feet were getting very cold, so I went inside.

They *were* getting used to me. They *were* keeping a less-close eye on me. I might be able to just *walk myself out of here* when it warmed up. Maybe.

In March, Joy's pregnancy would reach thirty-seven weeks; Bethany would turn fourteen and be handed over to Ethan as a "wife."

March weather was wildly unpredictable. But if I had an opening, I was going to have to try.

CHAPTER 8

On a Thursday in early March, I heard the wind blowing outside and expected a blast of cold when I came out of my cabin. Instead, I was greeted with a blast of unseasonably pleasant dry air: a Chinook. Warm, dry air coming down the east side of the mountains, due to some weird weather thing that my father had explained to me when we'd had a Chinook in Minot when I was a kid.

The magical thing about Chinooks is the fact that they don't just melt snow, they sublimate it: the air is so dry and warm the snow goes directly from solid to gaseous state. Well, some of it does, anyway. The Chinook also raises the air temperature very rapidly, and after breakfast I left my coat unzipped and my hood back. It wasn't quite T-shirt weather but it was stunningly, delightfully warm.

Which meant maybe I could make a run for it. It was still March, and once the Chinook stopped blowing, the cold would quickly return, so it would be risky. But if I wanted to get out of here in time to send someone back to rescue Joy, and Bethany, this might be my only chance.

Unfortunately, Sarah seemed as aware as me that at the moment, they couldn't count on the fear of freezing to death in the woods to keep me from fleeing: she would not let me out of her sight. She sat with me at breakfast, followed behind me within easy grabbing range when I went to get a second cup of coffee, escorted me to the clinic, rang the bell for one of the men to escort me when I said during a break in patients that I wanted to go back to my own cabin to shed my thermal underwear. She did let me go to the bathroom without her, but when I examined the clinic's bathroom windows, I discovered that they were unopenable glass block. Someone would probably have noticed me climbing out, anyway.

My cabin bathroom had no windows at all, but the cabin itself did, next to my bed. That night I checked the window and discovered it had recently been nailed shut. This made me wonder if there was something on the door itself that notified the man standing guard at night that I'd opened my door. Probably yes. Could I disable it? Or would that just tip them off that I'd found it?

I stepped outside. The night guards no longer asked me why I'd come out, they all just assumed it was a hot flash, but tonight Elmo, the man standing guard, came straight over and just watched me, silently. Eventually I went back inside and lay down, staring up at my dark ceiling.

Maybe part of why they were so worried was that Joy was almost due. Maybe they were all worried that I'd get away, and leave Joy without medical support. Of course, she wouldn't be without medical support; I was *absolutely* calling the police the minute I was out of here! But they might not think of it that way. They might assume they'd catch me if I tried to run. And murder me and bury me next to the other doctor.

And they didn't want to do that until I'd done Joy's C-section.

Friday morning in the mending corner, Natalie measured Bethany for her wedding dress. Bolts of white bridal fabrics were leaned against the wall, and she asked Bethany to pick her favorite of a shiny satin and a matte satin. Bethany stroked both fabrics, her brow furrowed, and said, "They're both beautiful, ma'am. Either is fine."

After Natalie had finished taking her measurements, Bethany was invited to sit down and work on mending for a bit at her mother's side. Heather talked about how while of course the reason for this was tragic, it was convenient that Brother Ethan had a house of his own already and they hadn't had to build the newlyweds a house. When Brother Nick and little Chloe—Sister Chloe, she corrected herself—when Chloe came of marriageable age, they'd had to wait an extra six months because some of the materials for their house hadn't come.

I looked at Emma, who was nodding and laughing with everyone else.

Joy came out of the kitchen with one of the big cans of corn. "Sister Emma," she said accusingly. "One of the cans you brought home on your last shopping trip has gone bad. It's *foul* inside."

"I'm terribly sorry, Sister Joy," Emma said. "But this is hardly my fault. It's not as if I could open it up and take a sniff before I brought it home."

Joy thrust the can at Emma and said, "It was the last can. It's spoiled, it will make everyone sick if it goes into dinner, and without it, there won't be enough."

Emma stood up, indignant. "Go get Brother Jason," she said. "We'll run into town and buy some small cans, it's not the end of the world. Bethany, go get my coat, I left it in the house this morning." She stalked out.

Heather went to find Jason, and Janet volunteered to go ask Pastor for the debit card. Suddenly there were a lot fewer people there to watch me, although unfortunately one of them was Natalie.

"It's not as if we'll all starve without corn in the taco soup," Natalie said.

"Tell that to the men working a full day on the ranch," Joy snapped.

Something was odd about this whole interaction; I had never seen Joy act like this. Was she going into early labor? It wouldn't even be all that early, at this point. "Joy, you should probably sit down," I said. "Maybe come to the clinic with me for an exam? I'm worried about you."

She shot me a brief, guarded look, and I was suddenly certain that this was a distraction of some kind, that a plan was underway that I wasn't part of, and I had no idea whether pressing for a trip to the clinic, or pressing for her to lie down right here, or just letting her continue to throw an uncharacteristic tantrum over spoiled corn was the thing that would get her what she needed. *That would get Bethany what she needed*, I thought, realizing why Emma had sent Bethany out ahead of her.

"What's going on? I heard you were upset, Sunshine." Pastor John had arrived at the mending corner.

"The corn is spoiled, and there won't be enough soup tonight, and Daddy, I am so tired and I was so looking forward to the taco soup," Joy said, standing up and awkwardly throwing herself into the pastor's arms and pressing her face to his shoulder.

David had come in behind him, and looked around the mending circle. I hadn't been introduced to Joy's husband, but he was often invited to do the daily Bible reading, and I'd heard people talk about him. I'd have recognized him as Calum's brother from the patchy blond beards they both sported, in any case. "Pastor, send me to town with Brother Jason. Let Sister Emma get back to her mending. She should be able to spend this time with her daughter. Where is Bethany, by the way?"

"Getting Sister Emma's coat," Natalie said. "She left it behind this morning, it's so warm out."

Joy pulled away from her father, rubbing her eyes. "I'm sorry for making a scene, Daddy."

"As you should be, Sunshine. But we'll get you your corn. Why don't you go home and rest? Someone else can take over in the kitchen."

I stood up. "I'm not an expert cook, but I can chop things, if that's what's needed."

I was hoping that shifting from my expected job (mending) to something less standard would help me slip my watchers, but I should have known better: Sarah was working in the kitchen, and had me come stand right by her to peel and dice carrots.

If I'd had a watch, I could have at least timed how long the trip to and from town took Jason and David. It wasn't a five-minute drive, though, that much was clear; it was at least a fifteen-minute drive, maybe longer. When they came back, Jason brought the bag of cans into the kitchen and laid out ten regular-sized cans of corn, and David went to a cabinet, unlocked it, and hung something inside.

Hung a *key* inside. David was carrying a padlock-type key, but what he'd just put away was the minivan key. The key to the minivan was stored in a locked cabinet in the kitchen.

THE TACO SOUP WAS lunch, and I spent it thinking about that locked cabinet.

It did not look like a particularly sturdy cabinet. It looked like the kind of cabinet I could get into with a crowbar, if I had a crowbar. Or the claw part of a claw hammer. I probably would need a tool well suited to prying things, though; I didn't think a butter knife would do it, which was a shame because I had regular access to butter knives. Had I ever seen a crowbar here? I probably hadn't, but if I started keeping my eyes open, maybe I would spot one.

"Thank you for going to get the corn," Emma said to David, who was sitting near me at the table.

"Happy to do it," he said, not looking up.

Emma had arranged to send Bethany to meet her at the minivan, on what I was pretty sure had been a planned escape attempt. She surely hadn't intended to leave JJ here. Heather had gone to find Jason, and Janet had gone to find Pastor John; one of them had probably made a detour to wherever JJ was, to send him to meet the minivan. I wondered which of them was in on the plan. Or if both of them were. Or if neither of them were and getting JJ had been Jason's job. Or, hell, Bethany's. Just because I thought Bethany might spill my secrets to the cult didn't mean her mother did.

If I could slip my *please call my father* note to Emma, that might be all it took. But when we reassembled for more mending after lunch, Emma was nowhere to be seen. She had been sent off to work in the laundry room, instead.

When I stepped out after dinner, the wind had died down and the temperature was rapidly falling. I could smell snow in the air. I'd had a window, but that window had closed. I was going to have to keep waiting.

ANOTHER WEEK PASSED. ANOTHER foot of snow fell. Natalie made a floor-length, high-collared, long-sleeved white dress for Bethany, and had her put it on for a fitting. Emma was still working in the laundry, but the rest of the mending corner told Bethany that she would be a beautiful bride.

Her birthday, I'd found out, was the fifteenth. Her wedding was scheduled for the sixteenth.

"We should do a physical exam," I said one day when Bethany was in the clinic and no other patients had arrived. "Make sure there isn't any reason you can't safely carry a child."

Sarah gave me a suspicious glare. "You examined Bethany just last month."

"I did not realize last month that Bethany would be getting married in March. Perfectly healthy for a young teenager does not necessarily mean fully ready for pregnancy and birth."

Sarah granted what was clearly reluctant permission. I weighed Bethany again, measured her, and drew blood to check for anemia. Pelvimetry is a technique of measuring a woman's pelvis to estimate whether it's likely to allow a baby to pass through at birth; the thing is, I was pretty sure that Bethany would find even a regular pelvic exam traumatic, and I also did not think Sarah would allow me to perform one. I settled for an abdominal ultrasound followed by saying that Bethany's pelvis was insufficiently developed to support a pregnancy and she needed to wait at least a year.

"A woman's body won't grow a baby that's too big for her to deliver," Sarah said, serenely, which is a line you'll sometimes hear from natural birth advocates. (It is straight up not true.) "The position of the baby is the most important factor in natural birth, and if need be, you can perform a C-section."

If there'd been any Depo-Provera in the cabinet, I'd have been tempted to try to give Bethany the shot, to at least buy time before she could get pregnant. But there wasn't; also, Sarah was watching me very closely today.

Bethany was overall in good health. If she'd arrived in my office pregnant, due to consensual sexual activity with a boy her actual age, I'd have gone down the list of risks to be aware of, warned her that girls her age were more likely to give birth prematurely, referred her to resources for teen mothers, and expected things to probably go fine. What appalled me here was the knowledge that she hadn't chosen this, the adults around her had chosen this, and she was going to be forced to go through a pregnancy while still absolutely a child, and there was nothing I could do to stop it.

One week before Bethany's birthday, overnight, I woke to a loud, urgent knock at my door. I got up and found myself face-to-face with Joy, in a nightgown with boots underneath and an unzipped coat over top. Calum had been standing guard overnight and was trailing after her. "You're supposed to go to the clinic and have me get—" he was yelling.

"Hello, Sister Joy," I said. "Is everything okay?"

"I think I'm having contractions," she said. "I mean, I think they're different."

Calum's face was flushed with fury; he grabbed her arm and she shook him off. "Brother Calum!" she said. "You're not to touch me, I am David's wife!"

"Then you should be *listening* to me!" he snapped. He wasn't reaching for the gun slung over his shoulder, but I was suddenly, acutely aware of its presence. I straightened my spine, cleared my throat, and gave him a long, steady glare. He was young enough I thought this *might* work, and in fact, he fell back a half step. "Sister Joy, I am going to go get Pastor. *And* Brother David. *And* Sister Sarah," he said.

"Of course," I said. "Sister Joy, I need to change into scrubs, so why don't you sit down while I do that." Calum had fallen back just enough to let me close my door on him; I turned to Joy, who wordlessly grabbed my hand. I could feel the crinkle of paper against my palm. Her face was blotchy and as I watched, she bent over with a gasp. Real contractions, all right.

"Sit," I said. "I'll get my scrubs on as fast as I can. How long have you been having these?"

"I don't know," she said, her voice rough. "I mean, I've *been* having contractions. When I realized these were different, I realized they'd been different for a while. It crept up on me."

I leaned into my wardrobe to pull out scrubs, and unfolded the note.

> There's a plan to get out of here but my surgery is the distraction. You have to make it last as long as you can. They'll tell someone about you they promise. Please don't tell.

I wondered how many women were in on this plan. Or maybe it wasn't just women? Jason was probably in on it. I tucked the note into my bra next to my other notes, then changed into scrubs as fast as I could. "Let's go," I said, but the door banged open before we could leave. Pastor John strode in, with Joy's husband David at his heels.

At the sight of her father, Joy dissolved into silent, fearful sobs. "I'm worried about the baby, Daddy," she gasped. "I think it might be coming. It's too early, isn't it? It's so early."

The pastor's anger faded and was replaced with exasperation. "What do you think Doc Elizabeth is going to be able to tell you from *here*, Sunshine? It's her house, it's where she *sleeps*. You're supposed to have her meet you at the *clinic*."

"I don't mind," I said, mustering as much good cheer as I could, surrounded by cold air and angry men. "Let's just all go over together." I turned to Brother David and swung straight into the patter I used when meeting a father who hadn't come to the prenatal appointments. "You must be Brother David, Sister Joy's husband! It's a pleasure to meet you. You must be so excited. Are you nervous at all? Because that's as normal for fathers as it is for mothers, especially with a first baby."

"Not really," he said. "I mean, I'm not nervous. I guess I'm excited." He glanced over at Pastor John.

I had a little speech I'd given a few times to husbands with male-factor infertility who'd confessed, or made me think they wanted to confess, that they were afraid their donor-conceived child wouldn't feel like theirs. *You will be the father in every way that matters. You are going to look at this baby and see your son. He's going to look at you and see his daddy. It will be okay, I promise.* I didn't get the sense that David would be a receptive audience. I tried not to think about what Joy had just told me, that maybe—maybe!—someone would escape and send back help.

It was snowing: wet, heavy snow mixed with rain. If anyone was going to try to walk to safety, I hoped they knew what they were doing. I led the way over to the clinic, where Sarah had unlocked the door and turned on the lights. "We'll take good care of you," she said to Joy.

Joy was definitely in labor. "Do you think we should do the steroid shot for her?" Sarah asked. "Hold off delivery for a day?"

That might not be optimal for the escape. *I can't think about that now; I have to think about the patient in front of me.*

Joy grabbed my hand. "We can't wait," she said. "I think you need to get this baby out of me, and I think you need to do it *now*," she said. "God put it on my heart"—she broke off with a groan of pain—"God put it on my heart that this baby needs to be born tonight. *Tonight*."

Sarah looked at me.

"Maternal instincts are a powerful indicator," I said. This was not actually clinically true, and I hoped it did not come back to bite me. "We're going to need an ultrasound to look at fetal positioning, though, given Joy's uterus."

"You said *tonight*, right, Joy?" Sarah said. "It's just after midnight, there's a whole lot of *night* left." She rolled the ultrasound machine over. The baby was still transverse, which was not surprising. But the heartbeat looked nice and strong, and I actually had a pretty good feeling about lung development. This baby was *almost* term.

"Okay," I said. "Okay. I can perform the C-section tonight. Sarah, are you doing the surgical assisting?"

"We have someone else for the surgical assisting. Brother Mike."

"How did no one tell me this before?" I snapped. "Guess you'd better get him in here, then." Sarah ran to the door and actually ran *out* to find Mike, leaving me briefly alone with Joy.

I leaned down and whispered, "Are you sure about this?"

She whispered back, "Make it last as long as you can. If you can take my whole goddamn uterus out and burn it, so much the better."

Sarah was back, Mike in tow, Bethany at his heels. "Howdy, Doc," he said.

Joy visibly jerked when she saw Bethany. “I don’t want the child here,” she said.

Bethany’s face visibly fell, but I leapt to agree. “Bethany, this is a surgery; you can’t be here for a surgery, not yet. When you’re fourteen—” I issued the promise recklessly. “We’ll train you for surgical assisting and you can be at surgeries once you’re fourteen.” I could feel Joy relax slightly beside me. “For now, Brother Mike, get into scrubs. There’s a bathroom over there. While you’re scrubbing up, tell me what your actual experience is.” Mike turned out to be trained as a veterinary assistant, so normally he did this on *literal farm animals*, but at least he probably wouldn’t faint at the sight of blood. “Are you even going to know what the instruments are called when they’re for humans and not for cows?”

“Oh, yeah,” Mike said. “They’re mostly called the same things. I checked.”

I decided that if anything went wrong, I was going to try to throw the blame on Mike. Sarah got out masks, gloves, laid out autoclaved surgical instruments. Up at the meal hall I could hear a bell tolling. “What’s that for?”

“A prayer vigil to welcome Pastor’s first grandson,” Sarah said.

I looked at Joy, who didn’t seem alarmed, so probably that was part of the plan. Sarah pulled out the anesthetics and I set to work delivering the largest and longest-lasting dose of spinal anesthesia I could do.

I HAVE DONE OVER a thousand C-sections in my career as an ob-gyn. I’ve overseen many more vaginal deliveries. (I’ve *done* exactly zero of those, personally—the woman delivers the baby, with a normal childbirth. The doctor's just there to catch. And I've never given birth myself.) I have performed hysterectomies, rectocele repairs, tubal ligations, oophorectomies.

Those didn't prepare me for this. Even my rotation in Haiti did not prepare me for this. Well, that's not *entirely* fair, because obviously I brought my normal skill set to this horrifying, absurd situation. What I drew on more, though, was the time back during my residency when I and two surgical residents, near the end of a very long shift, went down the rabbit hole of Leonid Ivanovich Rogozov, a doctor on an Antarctic expedition in 1961 who removed his own appendix under local anesthetic. We'd all found it fascinating and had argued about which surgical tasks we might reasonably walk a non-doctor through, if any, and whether we could use a camera to better effect than Rogozov's mirrors. (He had set up mirrors, but gave up on using them partway through and did the surgery by touch.)

Operating in a makeshift operating theater with a surgical assistant who'd only ever practiced on animals: a piece of cake compared to doing your own appendectomy. They hadn't skimped on the lighting, so I could see what I was doing. Joy closed her eyes tight, doing her best impression of a woman under general anesthetic.

The table—such as it was—was the wrong height, and my back started cramping almost immediately. No matter how well Bethany had sanitized this room, she was a child, and we weren't in a hospital; Joy's infection risk was going to be appalling.

The baby was a boy, small but breathing on his own. In addition to Mike the vet tech, Janet had been standing by, ready to take charge of the baby. I didn't ask what pediatric training she'd had—that wasn't my problem, and I needed to focus on Joy.

Normally, a C-section takes about forty-five minutes, if nothing goes wrong; it's stitching that takes the most time. But even aside from Joy's directive to make the surgery take as long as possible, I was working under strange and stressful circumstances. I'd counted instruments and sponges before starting, and I counted them all four times before I closed. I'd never done a surgery with a retained surgical item, and this would be a very bad time to start.

The thing about making surgery take longer is that it also makes infection risk higher. Fortunately, once the fascia is closed, that risk drops precipitously and there's still quite a lot to do. I started by closing the fascia with a lot of attention to perfect hemostasis, trying to fix every last capillary. Once that was done, I deliberately slowed down even more. "This is taking a lot longer than it does when you repair a tear," Sarah remarked.

Joy's eyes screwed shut even tighter, but she didn't need to worry; I reached for my "training the new residents" voice. "A recent study found that the best suturing technique for perineal injuries is continuous, nonlocking sutures. That means something like a running stitch. Whereas with cesarean surgery, I like my scars to be perfect, and the simple interrupted suture, like I am performing here, is one of the best ways to provide a small, minimally noticeable scar. The running stitch does take less time, which is kind of a nice bonus for everyone, but the main reason I use it on perineal tears is that it results in significantly less pain for the patient." Lecturing slowed me down even more, so as I continued working, I lectured Sarah and Mike on things to watch for that might indicate trouble or complications, and I had them give her some pain medication so that she wouldn't get slammed with surgical pain the instant the spinal wore off. Joy didn't object, which I hoped meant she wasn't required to be clearheaded for the plan to come off.

I'd finished closing Joy but was still lecturing Sarah and Mike when David burst in.

"Where's the baby?" he shouted. "Where's my son?"

"Sister Janet took him," Sarah said. "I assumed—didn't she bring him back to your place? He's fine, he's healthy. She was—she was going to bathe him. She couldn't do that here." She gestured to the clinic-turned-field-hospital, at the harsh lights and the tight space.

I sat down, still in my scrubs, on a chair that had been pushed into the corner. I had not realized that the plan had included taking Joy's child. That seemed risky. Riskier. Next to me, Joy stirred. Normally—in a hospital—patients who'd just had a C-section were taken off to recovery to be monitored by nurses as the anesthesia wore off, but obviously that wasn't going to happen here. Joy whimpered a little.

"He *must* be somewhere," Sarah was saying.

"I'm telling you, he's *gone*. We can't find Janet, either."

Joy opened her eyes.

"You have a healthy son," I told her. "How do you feel?"

"Where's my baby?" Joy whispered.

"He's doing great," I said, hoping this was true and hoping that Joy remembered the plan, if this had been part of the plan. "Do you want to see your husband?"

She shook her head. “I want to see my baby,” she said. “Oh. It hurts. What did you do to me? It *hurts*.”

“Sarah,” I said, interrupting the conversation. “Give Joy another five milligrams of morphine, please.”

“Joy?” David said, coming around to bend down over her. “Where’s my son?”

“How is Joy going to know the answer to that question?” I said, trying to put myself between them. “She’s been *a surgical patient* for most of the last *two hours*.”

“Get out of the way,” David growled at me.

I pulled myself straight. “You need to leave my patient alone. I don’t care if she’s your wife.”

“David?” Joy said. “Where’s the baby? What happened? Where is he?”

There was a long silence, and then David turned on his heel. “We’ll find them,” he said. “They can’t have gone far.”

I stepped outside. The night was nearly over, and the compound was full of activity. There’d been a prayer vigil and sleepy children who’d spilled out of the community building were now being herded back in. Holly was hurrying past me with her head down. “What’s going on?” I called to her, and she looked up at me, her face distracted.

“Brother Jason and Sister Emma are missing,” she said. “Along with their children. And no one knows where Sister Janet took Sister Joy’s baby.”

Pastor John was unlocking the building where they kept the vehicles. “The minivan’s still here,” I heard him call. “And the truck. The Gator’s gone.”

“I’ll get the keys,” David snarled, and ran up to the

community building. He was back a minute later, shouting for Brandon. Apparently he'd used the minivan for the feed pickup today because the pickup wasn't running, and the keys were still in his pocket, instead of in the cabinet. There was a spray of gravel as David whipped the minivan out of the garage. "Brother Ethan—"

"Yes, of course," Ethan said. He climbed in, his rifle across his lap, and the minivan roared away up the driveway into the dark.

Sarah came out of the clinic, white-faced. "Go sit with Sister Joy," she said to me.

In the clinic, Sarah had shut off the bright lights. The sheets around Joy were still stained with her blood—even a surgery that goes well produces a certain amount of blood. Joy was asleep; Sarah had given her a pillow for her head. The second bed in the clinic had been folded up and shoved into one of the closets to make more space for the surgery. I brought it back out and made it up, thinking that when Joy roused I could move her over to the clean, unbloodied bed.

I'm a good doctor, but I'm really not much of a nurse. Postoperative care at this point was solidly in the nursing domain, and if I'd shown up in a patient's room post-cesarean to sit with her, get her up and walking, and help her initiate breastfeeding, the nurses would have made it extremely clear that I was overstepping. (There are doctors who will tell you that the nurses aren't supposed to yell at you. Let me just assure you that nurses do not *have* to raise their voices to let you know you're out of line and in their way.)

Sarah, though, was off hunting for Janet, so Joy had me. And I wound up just sitting down, exhausted, on the second bed, because I realized looking at the empty vial in the trash that Sarah had given her enough morphine to thoroughly knock her on her ass; she wasn't going to be up and walking for a while yet.

So. Jason and Emma had taken Bethany and JJ—along with Janet, and Joy's baby—and made a run for it. They'd taken, of all vehicles, the golf cart. I thought they'd probably planned on the minivan, only to be unable to get the keys because they were in Brandon's pocket. If they'd taken the minivan, they'd be in town by now.

I wondered how fast the Gator went.

This would have been a much better plan if they *hadn't* taken Joy's baby. I wondered if this had been one of the conditions Joy set, to have her baby removed to safety? Or if this was a byproduct of Janet being the person who was supposed to take charge of the infant, and Janet wanting to leave?

But it had been an hour and ten minutes from the time Janet left with the baby to the time David had taken off in the minivan. That might have been enough time for them to get to town. To safety. It probably depended on how quickly they'd given up on finding the minivan keys.

In the distance, somewhere far from the compound, I heard a single gunshot.

My whole body went cold. Immediately outside, I could hear nothing. Everyone had heard the gunshot; everyone was waiting. *It might have been some nearby rancher taking out a wolf*, I thought, knowing that I was lying to myself and doing it anyway because there was no point in letting myself freak out until it was really, truly time to freak out.

Outside, the sky had lightened to the gray twilight

of just before sunrise. I heard the sound of the minivan coming back.

I stepped outside the clinic and David climbed out, Joy's infant in his arms. Ethan had been driving, and he came around to fling open the sliding door; he yanked Emma out by the hair and shoved her to the ground, where she huddled, her face a rigid, ashen mask. Jason climbed slowly out after her, and Bethany and JJ followed. Bethany was sobbing, big noisy sobs, and clutching JJ's hand.

Pastor John walked slowly down the gravel path toward them.

Jason dropped to his knees. "I gave in to temptation," he said, his voice shaking. "I put myself in the hands of the Elders for discipline. Emma—Emma was faithful. All she did was obey me, the fault is mine, not hers. I led my family astray."

I did not see Janet, and tried not to think about why she wasn't here.

Some of the older men stepped forward and took Jason by the elbows. "Emma, you should go back to your cottage with the children," one of them said. "Pray for your husband."

"Not her," Brother Ethan said, as Emma started to lead Bethany away. "You're not pouring any more of your poison into my wife's ears." He grabbed Bethany by the arm.

"She's not your wife yet. She's thirteen. She's a child!" Emma said.

Bethany clung to her mother with one hand and her brother with the other and looked from face to face. "Dr. Liz," she choked out. "Can I stay with you and Sister Joy?"

"Go to Dr. Liz," Emma whispered, and let go of Bethany's hand. She yanked her arm free from Ethan's grip and ran to me. I wrapped my arms around her; she was shaking. I led her back into the clinic and let her sit on the clean bed. There was a plug-in electric kettle in the corner, which I filled and started; Bethany needed to be treated for shock, and we had some herbal tea in a drawer that Sarah liked to bring out for prenatal visits. Once she'd calmed down slightly I could distract both of us by talking about postnatal care.

David came striding in, Sarah at his heels. I did not trust him with Joy. I didn't trust *any* of these people with Joy. But David seemed calmer now, with his son in his arms. He sat down on the bed beside her.

Joy was still sleeping off the morphine. David rocked the baby gently as I silently made a cup of tea for Bethany. Gray dawn light was coming in through the clinic windows, and I could hear a drone again, outside. Joy stirred slightly, and David nudged her. She roused. "Do you want to see our son?" he asked.

She shook her head, still half asleep. "No," she murmured. "Janet was going to take him to safety."

David looked at her, and then looked at me. And then gently handed the infant to Sarah, stood up, and grabbed my arm in an iron grip.

"No!" Sarah shouted. "We need her! We need a doctor, David!"

"Don't tell me she had nothing to do with this," he snarled. "I saw the look on her face, she *knew*. She was in on it!"

"Brother David, it is a risk every time we take someone. It is a huge, huge risk, we could get caught, we could bring Harvest to ruin, it's not *safe*. You have got to just leave her be! She's the reason you have a healthy baby. Sister Joy will *never* be able to deliver naturally, ever, you know that, she *has to have a doctor.*"

David looked down into my face, and shook his head. "Come on, Dr. Elizabeth."

"What, so you can shoot me like your last doctor?" I said.

He glanced over my shoulder at the child huddled on the second bed. "You don't want to make me do this in front of Bethany, do you?"

"We need to discuss this with Pastor," Sarah said. "Please, Brother David, I am begging you, we can surely discuss this with Pastor."

There was a crash as Bethany's mug hit the floor. "No," Bethany said. "No no no no no no *no.* Help, somebody, help us, don't let Brother David hurt Dr. Liz, somebody stop him!" Her voice rose from a protest to a shrill, urgent scream.

The door to the clinic burst open and I turned toward the door, hoping it wasn't Ethan, thinking perhaps it would be Pastor John, and maybe he would intervene, as Sarah clearly thought he would.

Instead, it was a man I didn't recognize. He wore goggles, hunter's camo, a bulky bulletproof vest, and he had a gun trained on all of us. David let go of my arm and turned toward the stranger, a look of fear on his face. "Who are you?"

If David didn't know who this man was, he must not be part of the cult. I flung my hands up and screamed, "Help, I'm a prisoner here! Please help me!"

The man in camo shoved David to the side; another

man came up behind him and peered through his goggles at my face. "Lizzie?" he said.

"Yes," I said. "Yes, that's me!"

He ducked his head to talk into a walkie-talkie clipped to his tactical vest. "Gwinn!" he said. "Found your kid!" He turned back to me. "Come on, we're getting you out of here."

I grabbed Bethany by the hand and stepped outside. There were cars—multiple cars. Multiple people, dressed in hunter's camo, carrying guns.

And my father, who came around one of the cars and grabbed me in a fierce hug.

"Dad," I said. "You found me."

"Of course I found you," he said. "I just needed a little help."

CHAPTER 9

"IS THERE ANYTHING HERE you need?" my dad asked.

"You have to help Joy," I said. "And her baby—and Emma and Jason—Bethany!" I looked around wildly for Bethany—she'd been right behind me—and saw her running to her cottage. "That girl there, she's just thirteen, she needs to come. Her whole family needs to come."

"Is this your coat?" The man who'd found me was walking over with it. "What happened to that woman in there?"

"That's Joy, she's my patient," I said. "She's just had surgery."

"We'll secure this place," the man said to my father. "You can get her back to Idaho Falls."

I grabbed my father's arm. "You have to find Bethany's father. Her family was trying to escape and they got caught—"

"Liz, we should get you out of here," Dad said.

"I think I found them," one of the other men called. "Are you Emma? Good news, you're all coming with us, I guess."

"And Joy," I said again. "But she's just had surgery." I pointed at the minivan, which still had its headlights on and all its doors open. "Someone's got the key to that minivan. If you put down all the seats you can let Joy ride lying down. And her baby! Don't leave her baby here!"

"Do you trust us to take care of this?" Dad asked.

"They've got guns, please be careful," I said.

"That's why I *really want to get you out of here*, Liz!"

"Okay," I said. "Okay." I didn't see Pastor John anywhere. "Also, there's this guy, Pastor John, he's in charge—"

We heard a gunshot.

"Get her out of here, now!" one of the men in camo shouted. "Move in, move in!"

My dad shoved me into one of the waiting cars, and the person at the wheel took off.

THE ROAD WAS WINDING and bumpy. My father introduced the driver as his friend Tom. "How did you find me?" I asked. "Why—I guess I was expecting the FBI, if anyone. What happened?"

"I mean, I did *talk* to the FBI," my dad said. "I *started* there. First, they gave me the whole speech about how adults had the right to disappear—you probably remember that from when Courtney went off camping in a snit—and then they said they were looking into it, and then when your text showed up, they said it didn't narrow things down enough to know where you were. 'Idaho is kind of a big state,' that's the line I recall the agent saying."

Tom snorted derisively.

"But some of my buddies from the VFW were former drone pilots," he continued. "And you can just *buy* a drone, these days, or rent it. So we came out here and started looking for a compound like what you'd described."

"And you found me?"

"We actually found enough places like what you'd described we had to keep surveilling."

"Turns out Idaho is kind of a big state," Tom said.

"I'd started out thinking we'd find you and then give the information to the FBI to do the rescue, but we all kept talking and came around to thinking we should do it ourselves."

"The FBI has fucked up too many operations for me to trust them," Tom said. "I was afraid they'd let the cult take you hostage or something."

"And then today we heard the gunshot while surveilling. So we just moved in. What happened?"

"There was a group that tried to run away. Bethany's family, and also this woman, Janet. I think the people who went after them probably shot Janet." I leaned forward in my seat. I wasn't buckled in. That should probably worry me. "Can you have them look for her? Maybe—"

"Worth a try," Tom said, and pulled up his radio. "Transport to Ops, you hearing me, over."

"Ops to Transport, loud and clear, over," a voice came back.

"Casualty reported somewhere along the road. The other noncombatants may have more information. Can you stop and render aid? Over."

"Roger that, Transport. We heard that from the other noncombatants and stopped to check. Unfortunately the casualty was shot in the head at close range and is past the point of rendering aid. We left her undisturbed because it's a crime scene. Over."

"Is Bethany okay?" I asked.

"Ops, can you confirm that Bethany is safe and in good health? Over."

Another pause. "Bethany sends the following message: I'm just fine, Dr. Liz, praise God. Over."

I sat back in my seat. I buckled my seatbelt.

My dad grabbed my hand and squeezed it.

"I still can't believe you found me," I said.

"It's because of your message," Dad said. "Once I had your message, I'd have found you if I'd had to *walk* every inch of Idaho. I just needed to know where to start looking."

IDAHO FALLS HAD AN FBI office.

"Do you feel up to making a report?" Dad asked. "I've got a local lawyer who'll go with us. I know you don't believe in talking to law enforcement without a lawyer."

"It really ought to be different when I'm the *victim of a crime*," I muttered.

"Bear in mind, my friends held them all at gunpoint to get you out."

"Yeah. Lawyer's a good idea. But I'm willing to go talk to the feds. There are a couple of people who absolutely need to be prosecuted."

"Do you want to go to a hotel first? I have some of your clothes, and other stuff from your apartment."

"My apartment, oh my God—"

"I took care of the rent, Liz, everything's right where you left it. One of your neighbors has been watering the plants, even."

"That seems really wasteful."

He scratched his chin. "I thought there might be clues I'd missed. That might help me find you. I didn't want to lose anything that turned out to be important, by packing it all up and putting it in storage."

The suitcase my father had brought along for me was a compact little case with the toiletries from my bathroom, four outfits, including a set of dress pants and a respectable-looking blouse, and—

I picked up my battered paperback copy of *The Onyx Dagger*. "How did you know to bring this?" I asked.

"You reread that book every time you get stressed out. I thought you might have recently been through a stressful experience. Your Kindle is in there, too. Do you want to take a shower? Your lawyer's on her way."

I TOLD THE FBI what had happened to me, with my lawyer, a nice woman named Beth Sheridan, at my elbow. We'd had a brief bonding moment over the whole "shared first name, different nicknames" thing. I kept having to remember not to call people *Brother* or *Sister* and slipped up, once, with Beth. As I got into the story of Joy's surgery, I realized I should talk to whatever obstetrician at the local hospital was caring for her now, because *surely* that person would have questions for me. The agent taking down my story called a break and said I should go to the hospital for a physical exam anyway.

"What's happening at the compound?" I asked.

"Law enforcement's on the scene," the agent said. "You'll get a full update later."

At the hospital, the ER doctor said I was in reasonably good health other than stress, and sent in a surgeon, who turned out not to be an obstetrician because they didn't have any obstetricians on staff. I told him the details of the surgery, and how Joy needed to be monitored closely for infection. They'd admitted her and the baby, and he reassured me that they'd be keeping an eye out for complications and transporting her to Spokane if anything came up.

I stepped out of the hospital with my father and lawyer and was briefly stunned by bright lights in the cloudy afternoon. "Dr. Gwinn!" someone was shouting.

"It's press, dammit," Beth muttered. "Just smile and wave." I followed her instructions and she shouted something promising a statement later. In the car back to the FBI office, she told me that I probably wanted to answer all the FBI questions first, then write a statement that she could deliver on my behalf. Or she could write it, if I wanted her to.

"Like . . . what sort of statement?"

"You appreciate all the well-wishes and concern and

would appreciate privacy while you recover from this very traumatic event," she said.

"I guess that's all true."

"Also, if you *do* want to give an interview, you should decide who you want to talk to and it can be a nice, calm chat, you don't want to yell answers out on the steps of the hospital. And you can expect money for it, if you want."

"What I want," I said, "is to make absolutely sure that my dad and his friends don't wind up in any trouble for *rescuing me.*"

It was well past dinnertime by the time we were all done being questioned and I could get an update. Most of the adults on the compound had surrendered, and lots of them were now saying they wanted help escaping and were being held against their will. Some of the questions the FBI had were to try to sort out which of them were *actually* fellow prisoners. Apparently Natalie, the woman who'd supervised the sewing circle, was one of the people claiming to have been held against her will, which seemed kind of rich to me. I had noted that Holly had a phone that she was using to send "all's well" texts, but Holly probably still had visible bruises from the beating due to that phone being found, so with a competent defense lawyer I thought she'd avoid jail time.

The body of the other doctor had been exhumed, and the FBI lab was working on her identity. Janet's body was in the custody of the medical examiner. Pastor John, Ethan, David, Sarah, and Brandon had all been arrested. Jason had disclosed that David had murdered Janet. All the men I'd seen with firearms were being held, including a few of the minor boys, and most of the children had been placed in emergency foster care while the system tried to figure out whether their mothers were victims or perpetrators.

But there hadn't been any more deaths after we left that day.

And it was over. I was safe.

My dad had gotten me a hotel room with a door that adjoined his, because he didn't want to let me out of his sight but thought maybe I'd like privacy. I hadn't managed to think about stopping anywhere for food, but one of Dad's buddies arrived minutes after us with a couple of bags of takeout: waffle fries, hot wings, stuffed mushrooms, and two burgers with Swiss cheese and mushrooms. We spread out the food on the little table by the window in Dad's room. Everything tasted amazing: the burger was rich and salty and chewy, the toasted bun crisp. There were *pickles*.

"They didn't feed you properly," Dad said. "You're thin."

"It was mostly just that the food there was really bad, but yeah, there also was never quite enough of it," I said.

To my relief, he didn't ask me any more questions; I'd spent the whole day answering questions and felt talked out. He told me all the family gossip I'd missed: one of my cousins was pregnant. Not the one who'd pulled the disappearing act, her sister. Their mother was finally selling her house, which was too big now that all the kids were grown, and hard to keep up; she'd found a condo, and was pressuring all her kids to take the "heirloom china," which was actually just 1980s-era wedding china. I could picture it as soon as Dad mentioned it, because I'd eaten Thanksgiving dinners off it on many occasions. It had butterflies on it, and back when I was ten, I had thought it was *beautiful*.

When I'd eaten all I could hold, I made sure both our hotel rooms were locked with the dead bolt and then left the door between our rooms ajar. I was exhausted—I'd been up most of last night with Joy, and then rescued, and then I'd spent the day talking to law enforcement. I put on the flannel pajamas Dad had brought in my suitcase—PJs instead of a nightgown—and brushed my teeth with my own brand of toothpaste for the first time in months. Finally I got into bed, propped myself with a mound of pillows, turned off all the lights but the one by my bedside, and reached for *The Onyx Dagger*.

> *The cold wind brought the smell of snow, and Deirdre, red-faced from the cold, paused in the stable yard, breathing in a deep breath of it. "My lady," the page said. "Your father said to send you in, directly." "Oh, I know," she said, giving him a quick smile. "I promise I won't delay much."*

You'd probably cough, I thought, if you took a big deep breath of cold air. I wondered if the author had ever thought about that, and then turned the page and kept reading.

I DREAMED ABOUT THE cult.

I was examining pregnant women, each with some

problem that was more horrifying and implausible than the last, like Natalie had placenta accreta that had somehow grown all the way through her abdomen and was protruding outside her body. "One more patient today!" Sarah said in her super cheerful voice, and the patient was Bethany, a very pregnant Bethany, who said in her sweet voice that everything was fine and Ethan was a faithful husband but looked at me with sad eyes that said *you let this happen, you let this happen to me.*

In my pocket, a phone rang; I pulled it out and answered it, and David's voice said, "You don't want to make me do this in front of Bethany, do you?"

I jerked awake, surprised by the silence of the room; the ringing phone had been so vivid I'd thought maybe I was hearing something real. It had been a *ring*, though, not a ringtone—a ring like phones had back in the landline era.

I got up and went to the bathroom and got a drink of water, trying to shift myself out of the dream space enough that the nightmare wouldn't pick up where it had left off once I went back to sleep. The bedside clock said it was 3:30 a.m., much too early to get up, but my heart was pounding now, and I switched on my bedside lamp to read some more of *The Onyx Dagger.*

I heard footsteps from the next room. "Lizzie?"

"I had a bad dream, Dad," I said. "Just going to read a little before I go back to sleep."

Dad nodded and sat down in the chair in my room. "I think it was the pickles that did it," he said.

I snorted a little and laid my book aside.

"They have medication for nightmares, just so you

know," Dad said. "I mean, I know you're a doctor, but I'm not sure if this is in your wheelhouse."

"This is the blood pressure med, right?" I said. "Not exactly my wheelhouse, but I remember a study making the rounds a while back."

"I was prescribed it for enlarged prostate, years ago now. I'd heard people say it could help with nightmares, but I didn't really expect it to work."

"Did it?"

"Not quite as well as I'd hoped, but more than I'd expected."

We were both quiet for a minute or two, and then I asked, "Did you have nightmares about Vietnam?"

"Of course I did." He paused, and then said, "When I first got back, I didn't talk about them with anyone. Your mom convinced me to talk to her, even if I had to wake her up in the middle of the night, and that helped, actually. Do you want to tell me about your nightmare?"

"Bethany was pregnant," I said. "It was my fault for not stopping it." Dad started to say something and I interrupted to go on. "Last month there was this woman, Holly. She got caught with a cell phone—the one I'd found and used to text you. I put it back in its hiding place, but it was found and they beat her and made us sing while they were doing it and I didn't say *anything*, Dad, I told myself it wouldn't matter but I didn't even *try* because I was so afraid they'd just beat me, instead. Or they'd beat her just as much and then beat me, too."

"Ever heard of moral injury?"

"Oh. Yes, actually." Moral injury is when your trauma

is compounded by being in a situation where you felt like your own actions were morally wrong.

"You know I was in combat search and rescue. Flying rescue missions in a prop plane. So in some ways I was lucky. It was a fucked-up war, but I had a mission that made sense to me."

"Yeah."

"But the day I had to eject, it wasn't actually because of antiaircraft fire, I just fucked something up and my engine cut out. I *almost* hit the ground before I could eject, but I made it out, and then had to hide and try to avoid being taken prisoner and wait for my own rescue mission. Someone from my own unit died trying to rescue me. Father of two. It felt like a bad trade."

"Is that what you dream about?"

"Sometimes. When your mother got cancer, though, I started dreaming that the cancer was my fault, that I'd given it to her. I didn't feel like I could talk to her about that, she'd feel like she needed to reassure me and she had enough to be getting on with. But fortunately the medication helped." He laughed a little. "I actually saw the doctor for the enlarged prostate because I was afraid all my nighttime bathroom trips might disturb her sleep. The drug felt like a miracle, honestly."

"If these keep up, I'll talk to someone."

"You should probably talk to someone regardless, you know?"

"When I get back to Minnesota," I said. It was hard to know what it would take to make me feel safe again. It was hard to know what would help. My room had two beds, and after a little while, Dad lay down on the other bed, instead of going back to his own room, and I turned off the light again and slept.

I'D HOPED I'D QUICKLY be on my way back to Minnesota, or at least Minot, but it turned out we were stuck in Idaho Falls for days. All of us: the cult, and also my father's group of friends, which he called the Task Force. They'd started out with a handful of people he knew from the VFW post in Minot, which meant mostly Air Force retirees. But as the plan had gotten more complex, they'd recruited friends from other branches. Tom was an Army vet who'd driven a truck in Mosul, and the guy I'd encountered on the porch was also former Army.

It was pretty clear that the FBI had a few *reservations* about how things had gone down: the Task Force's story was that they had just been working on finding me, that a full rescue was merely a backup plan in case time was of the essence, and then, in fact, time *was* of the essence (and I backed them up on this).

One of the younger and chattier members of the Task Force got a Facebook message from an old high school friend, saying, "Dude, is this *you*? What *happened*?" and told her his version of the whole thing. This high school friend—Matt admitted that he did *technically speaking* know this, he just hadn't thought about it until after the conversation—was a reporter at the *Kansas City Star*, so Matt's version of the story went very, very public, which set off a big round of speculation about whether his story was accurate, or if I had actually *joined* the cult and my father had talked everyone into helping him with a kidnapping and forceful deprogramming.

At that point I decided to talk to the press. I mostly hadn't, back when I was on trial, and although "don't talk to the press" was good advice to someone facing a felony charge, I found it profoundly annoying to be *talked about* instead of *listened to.* Beth set it up, and I spent an hour telling my story to a nice woman with good vibes as she sat with her hands folded in her lap, leaning forward occasionally to ask me for more details, while two people with lights and cameras focused on recording the conversation.

I watched a little snippet of that interview, and hearing my voice stopped me cold. It's always weird to hear your own voice recorded, but my voice sounded more wrong than it usually did. It sounded high. Sweet. *Gentle.* I didn't even know how to *begin* dealing with that, so I shut it off.

Some of the cult members who weren't behind bars also gave interviews. To hear them tell it, they'd all desperately wanted to escape starting at least a month or two before I was kidnapped, but had been unable to because of the cult's control over cars and phones. "We could have risen up and seized the means of production," I muttered, watching a tearful Natalie talk about how she was trapped. "You were watching *me*, Natalie! Who was watching you?"

It should not have surprised me to run into Joy, but it did.

I went into the diner with the all-day breakfast. It was the first day I'd gone anywhere at all without my father almost within arm's reach; I'd told him I wanted to try it, and he'd agreed to have his own lunch in one of the other restaurants on the block.

It took me a second to recognize Joy: she had gotten her hair cut into a bob. She saw me, though, and waved with a bright smile; as our eyes met, she seemed to suddenly realize that I might not want to see her, and put her hand down. She was in a booth, and there was a bucket car seat on the bench next to her.

I went over. "How are you doing?" I asked.

"Oh," she said, and looked sort of abashed. "The doctor said it was okay if I left the hospital. He said you'd done a really good job, he wouldn't have known from my recovery that it was a surgery done in a barn if no one had told him. That's what he said, I mean. In a barn."

I laughed. "Can I join you?"

"If you want to. I mean, yes, of course. Are we allowed to talk to each other?"

"No one's told me not to talk to you."

The waitress came by and dropped off a menu. "I know what I'm having," I said. I'd looked at the menu online. "I'd like a large coffee and the Belgian waffles with strawberries and whipped cream."

She glanced at Joy, who was finishing a Denver omelet. "Same check or different?"

Joy flushed. "I really feel like I ought to pick up your check, but I have exactly enough money to pay for my omelet and a tip."

"Separate checks," I said.

When the waitress had gone, Joy said, "I'm staying at a women's shelter, with Charlie. This is Charlie." She patted the carrier. "Charles means *free man*. I don't know where we're going from here, though. David's going to prison. My father, too. Well, maybe. He didn't shoot anybody."

"I expect they'll come up with something to charge him with," I said.

"Anyway, thank you," Joy said. "For everything. Delivering him, but also that text you sent. I heard from Emma that's how we got saved after I blurted out . . . ugh." She wiped her eyes. "I really did not mean to tell them anything. I'm usually so good at keeping quiet and not letting anyone know what I'm thinking."

"It wasn't your fault," I said. "You were just trying to survive the best you could."

"If we'd waited another day . . ."

"My dad's friends came in when they did because they heard the gunshot," I said. "And if I'd had the opportunity to run, I'd have done it. I didn't know if my father had gotten the text, I didn't know he was planning something. It had been weeks."

"I feel like you should know that it was *because of me* that they kidnapped you."

"I mean, I think I knew that? Did you *ask* them to get you a doctor?"

"Kind of."

"Normal people, if their wife or their daughter says, 'You have to get me a doctor,' take that person to a doctor. Like, they take them to a clinic or a hospital. Normal people do not *kidnap a doctor*."

"I knew they weren't normal people, though."

"You know what, Joy, I don't blame you, so just . . . please stop worrying about it. You've got enough going on." I nodded at Charlie, who was sleeping. "How's Charlie doing?"

"His pediatrician says he's doing really well, all things considered."

My waffles arrived and I dug in. Being able to *choose my own food* gave me a moment of delight, every time I sat down to eat. "Have you been reading since your escape?" I asked. "Like, for fun?"

Joy brightened up more than I'd ever seen her; it was like watching a sunrise. "*So many books*," she said. "There's a library here, and they've got *everything*. I told the librarian I wasn't sure where to start and she sent me home with one book from each section . . ."

We talked about books until Charlie woke up and our coffee was cold.

"I'll see you around," she said.

I nodded, even though I had my ticket back to Minneapolis. We'd see each other at the trial, at least. "Good luck." As we were walking out, I caught her arm. "Do you know where Bethany is?"

"She stayed with her parents. Everyone you insisted had to be brought out in the rescue, we were all treated as victims. So Bethany and JJ didn't go into foster care. They're staying at a family shelter run by the same folks as the women's shelter." She wrote down the address on the back of a placemat and gave it to me. "Are you going to go see her?"

"I don't know how she's feeling about everything. She might not want to see me," I said. "But there's something I want to give her, anyway."

THE FAMILY SHELTER HAD a check-in desk for visitors, it was not somewhere I could just wander in, so I told them

I was hoping to see Bethany. And maybe her parents, but mostly Bethany.

The receptionist paused and in even tones said, "Can you please tell me your relationship with this family?"

I realized she thought I was one of the cult members. I said, "I'm the doctor their cult kidnapped."

"Oh!" Her whole demeanor shifted. "Right. I'll go find Bethany."

"One other thing," I said. "If she doesn't *want* to see me, I don't want her to feel like she has to."

"I'll let her know that. Wait right here."

I could hear the pounding footsteps of someone running down the hallway and then Bethany *burst* out through the locked doors into the lobby. "Dr. Liz," she shrieked. Unlike Joy, she looked exactly the same: long red braids, long dress. When she flung her arms around me I did notice one thing, which was that the capacious pocket in her long skirt was now occupied by a paperback book.

Emma came out a minute later, saw us together, and quietly took a chair at the other end of the lobby. It was strange seeing her in blue jeans.

"How are you? I was so worried," Bethany said.

"Why were you worried?"

"Because they wouldn't let me see you! I was afraid you wouldn't ever want to speak to me again."

"Oh," I said. "No, Bethany, I'm not mad at you at *all*. I just had a lot of people I needed to talk to, and it didn't occur to me until today that I could just come find you. I wasn't sure if you'd want to see me, either."

"Of course I wanted to see you. Can I still be your apprentice?"

"Bethany." I took her gently by the shoulders. "You

will make an *amazing* obstetrician someday, if that's what you decide you want to do. But you will need to go to high school. And college. You'll have to do the pre-med requirements and apply to medical school, and go to medical school. And once you graduate from medical school, *then* you will be an apprentice obstetrician. And maybe, if I'm still practicing, you will get your residency at my hospital and I will train you. But probably you will learn from someone else. I'm sorry."

There was a long pause and then she said, her voice cracking a little, "That sounds really hard."

"You will do it one step at a time, just like I did. And maybe you'll decide you want to be a midwife instead of an obstetrician, or maybe you'll decide you want to do something completely different—it's your choice. But the first step is school. Your parents are going to have to send you to school." I glanced across the room at Emma, who lowered her eyes and gave me a quick, silent nod.

"We visited the school here yesterday," Bethany said. "But my dad wants us to move out of Idaho."

"That might not be a bad idea," I said. "But there will be a school wherever you go." I remembered the other thing I wanted to ask. "Did you see a dentist?"

"Yes, he gave me a filling." She opened her mouth and pointed. "And I saw an eye doctor and my new glasses work *so* much better. And JJ also saw a dentist and they pulled one of his teeth, but it was one of his baby teeth. The dentist said I needed braces but we're going to wait on those, my dad said, because we're maybe moving."

"I'm really glad you got the things you needed," I said.

She nodded. "If I'm not going to be your apprentice . . . can we still talk sometimes, at least?"

"Yes," I said. "Now that we're out of Harvest, we can use phones *or* email *or* we can send regular letters. And I wrote all my information down for you, in this. On the last page." I opened my bag and pulled out the paperback book I'd brought along.

Bethany's eyes went wide. "*The Onyx Dagger*! Is that the story you told me? It's a real book?"

"It is, in fact, a real book, and this is a real copy. And it's yours now." I laid it in her hands, reminding myself that other used copies existed *and also* I had the ebook. "You can read all the parts I forgot when I was retelling it. There were bunches, actually."

She gave me a last hug and then she and her mother went back in, Bethany's nose already in the new book.

ACKNOWLEDGMENTS

I swear standards for acknowledgments sections have gone up in the last five years. Instead of a straightforward set of paragraphs, they're long, detailed, poetic, *beautifully written*. Or maybe I'm just noticing the beautifully written ones more than I used to, who knows. It's my understanding that most regular readers don't actually read these, just writers who want to see if they're mentioned, or if they know anyone who's mentioned, or if they can suss out any interesting gossip. Anyway, I apologize in advance: these aren't going to be particularly poetic. Also I think the only gossip I share is old and pretty dull.

Anyway, I want to start by mentioning two books that helped me fill in some sense of what Liz's father might have experienced as an American pilot during the Vietnam War. I read *One Trip Too Many: A Pilot's Memoirs of 38 Months in Combat over Laos and Vietnam* by Wayne A. Warner, and *Cheating Death: Combat Air Rescues in Vietnam and Laos* by George J. Marrett. Marrett was the CSAR pilot who actually was told shortly after his arrival to just count himself as dead. I also want to thank Debra Freisleben for answering some questions about the Air Force by email.

I was extremely fortunate in having an *actual gynecologist* agree to read the whole manuscript. Noe Woods, thank you SO MUCH for your comments, which were extremely helpful. Any remaining mistakes are mine alone and were probably added to the manuscript after she saw it.

Thanks to my agent, Danielle Bukowski, for claiming me as a client when my previous agent departed (friends, I am on my *sixth* agent. It is normal for authors to have more than one agent over the course of their career but I am an outlier. There, that's the gossip I promised earlier) and for treating my work as worth the effort. Many thanks to Patrick Nielsen Hayden and Mal Frazier for their work on this book; to Patrick, for sitting me down in Glasgow and asking me to send him my next book; and finally, to Lydy Nickerson for reading Patrick and Teresa one of my short stories while on a road trip.

I have been a member of the Wyrdsmiths writers' group since 1997, and my friends and colleagues in the group remain indispensable to me as a writer and also, you know, because they're awesome and they're all friends I lean on for all sorts of reasons: Eleanor Arnason, Adam Stemple, Theo Lorenz, Kelly Barnhill, and Lyda Morehouse. Lyda is the friend who took over submitting my stories for me during the lowest point in my writing career and is also my best friend. Thank you, all of you.

My husband, Ed Burke, has always supported and believed in me. Ed, you're awesome and I love you. Thank you for everything.

And finally, my father, Bert Kritzer, to whom this book is dedicated. Liz's father, Sam, is not based on mine—my dad was a conscientious objector during the Vietnam War, to note one major difference. But Sam Gwinn got my dad's generosity, his problem-solving ability, and his fondness for long phone calls. (He also got my mother's anti-nostalgia for ice-cold outhouse seats.) Like Liz, I was deeply fortunate in my parents. Dad, thank you for your decades of support and encouragement. I love you.

CREDITS

Dear reader: you would probably not believe just *how many people* work on a book, unless you yourself are a writer or work for a publishing company. It's a lot. I have seen a couple of books now that have a credits section, like a movie does, and I like it, so I'm including one, because I want to express my deep appreciation for everyone who worked on this book. There were a lot of people.

Agent	Danielle Bukowski
Editors	Patrick Nielsen Hayden and Mal Frazier
Copyeditor	Shawna Hampton

Cover Designer	Katie Klimowicz
Interior Designer	Gregory Collins
Managing Editor	Lauren Hougen
Marketing Associate	Samantha Friedlander
Production Editor	Ryan T. Jenkins
Production Manager	Jacqueline Huber-Rodriguez
Proofreaders	Abby Colegrove and Lauren Hougen
Publicist	Saraciea J. Fennell

ABOUT THE AUTHOR

Richard Man

NAOMI KRITZER has been rereading favorite books since childhood, and probably still has passages from *A Wrinkle in Time* memorized. She writes for both adults and teens, including *Catfishing on CatNet*, *Chaos on CatNet*, and *Liberty's Daughter*. Her writing has won the Hugo Award, the Nebula Award, the Edgar Award, the Locus Award, and the Minnesota Book Award. Kritzer lives in St. Paul, Minnesota, with her family and three cats. The number of cats is subject to change without notice.